THE WEB

VOLUME TWO: FIGHTING BACK!

BY TOM HUGHES

Random House 🏠 New York

Library of Congress Catalog Number: 97-66665
ISBN: 0-679-87458-5
RL: 4.5

Printed in the United States of America 10 9 8 7 6 5 4 3 2 1

CHAPTER 1

DRIGOONAA

It was like a dream, but it wasn't a dream. Amy Rasmussen felt awake and asleep at the same time. She struggled to align her thoughts and memories.

It had been one month since the arrival of the Great Spiders. Enveloping the world in their sinister Web, the spiders had quickly taken over the major cities of the United States—and its people.

Once-bustling cities had been turned into virtual ghost towns, while what citizens were left had been transformed into zombies. Deeply entranced under the spell of the Great Spiders, these people were known as the webbed ones— so named because of the spider-web markings on their faces.

Only a lucky few had been able to escape the fate of becoming one of the webbed ones. With only each other to rely on, Amy and her friends, Stinky Elmo Dodd, Earl Two-Sticks, and Johnny Coombs, had banded together as the Spider-Killers, vowing to battle the spiders to the very end.

As Amy struggled to remember the recent events, she recalled the tunnels they had found underneath their school that had allowed them to escape the spiders.

She remembered meeting more rebels and learning from them about the control webs. Then she recalled how Johnny and Earl had gotten separated from her and Elmo.

"I remember all of that, but how did I get *here?*" Amy thought to herself. Then it all started to come back to her.

Just hours before now, she and the others had faced certain death as they stood helpless before the Great Spider that had cornered them. Its huge mandibles opened and shut, making the horrible clicking sound that meant "game over" to anyone who heard it.

At that moment, however, a form had flashed out of the woods and hurled itself at the Great Spider. It was another, smaller spider! All of a sudden, there were spiders fighting all around them—Great Spiders battling against the new, small spiders!

During the confusion as all the rebel humans fled for safety, Johnny and Earl were separated from her and Elmo. In the aftermath of this spider battle, one of the small spiders confronted Amy, who was tending to the unconscious Elmo. She remembered being strangely unafraid as the spider slowly put one of its spiked legs on her. Gently, the spider touched Amy's head.

Then she heard a voice.

The next thing Amy remembered was riding with Elmo "spiderback" through the forest. She felt as if she had been in some sort of a trance as she remembered the spider using one of its eight legs to help Amy lift the injured Elmo onto its back.

Do not fear me. You have the power to understand, the voice said as they traveled across the land.

Amy had understood the message, and she had believed it. After fifteen minutes of traveling, their journey came to an end in a dark cave. With horror, they realized that the cave was not a natural one—it was too even and smooth. And what was worse, they saw that they were surrounded by hundreds—maybe thousands—of spiders.

"Hi, everybody—nice place you've got here," Amy said suddenly, waving at the spiders. Not one of them, except the one that had brought them there, moved.

"You know," Elmo said, whispering to Amy, "these spiders might be able to conquer the world and junk, but I bet they're not much fun at parties."

Then they moved. A bunch of them approached and formed a ring around Amy and Elmo. Shuffling forward, the spiders raised their front legs, thrusting them into the air like spikes. Once again, they began to bring their legs down on Amy's head.

"Elmo!"

"Amy!"

Not enemy. Understand. UNDERSTAND.

The world exploded in a blast of white light. Amy couldn't see, but she wasn't blind—she knew instinctively that there was nothing to see. Elmo was near her—she could feel him. And she knew that he was feeling what she was feeling and that he wasn't afraid.

Then she had seen the Web. She could still see it now. Now she remembered everything.

Amy, can you see it?

It was Elmo!

Elmo, where are you?

Amy! I'm here.

Sure, but where is here?

I think we're—I don't know where we are. It sure is cool, though.

Stars shot past the kids at lightspeed. They felt themselves falling and flying at the same time. Visions of planets filled their eyes, and on every planet, giant spiders walked. They landed in huge ships, gleaming metal worlds filled with webs that carried, like computers, the whole history of the spider race.

We were proud, a voice said.

Who was that? Elmo asked.

Amy couldn't see her friend, but she felt that he was close to her. They were traveling together. How they were traveling, she wasn't exactly sure. Then, as if in answer to her unspoken question, the strange voice sounded once again in her ears.

You are traveling on the Web/Mind, it said.

Where are we going? Amy asked the voice.

Yeah, and what is going on, exactly? Elmo asked.

You will find out soon enough, the voice responded.

Suddenly, a planet loomed into view. Floating large and majestic against a backdrop of deepest purple-black, it was a planet of deserts, purple sand, and a red sky.

Drigoonaa, the voice informed them. **Our home world.**

Last stop, everybody out, Elmo said.

It's the home planet of the spiders. Why aren't I really, really scared? Amy said.

I'm not either. Maybe we're too dumb to be scared, Elmo said.

Speak for yourself, geek-brain... Amy began.

She had a lot more to say, but suddenly she couldn't speak or think. Any insults she had to throw at Elmo, who wasn't really all that bad, would have to wait until she got off this crazy ride, if she ever did. Somewhere, very far away, she could hear Elmo's voice calling for her. However, for some strange reason, she still wasn't afraid.

Amy's eyes fluttered open and she sat up. Her head hurt a little and she was very thirsty, but otherwise she felt all right. She looked around. Her eyes seemed to be a little out of focus. The walls of the room she was in, if that's what it was, looked gauzy and translucent. She shook her head, trying to clear her vision. The blurry quality of the walls persisted. It was as if someone had covered the rock walls of a cave with some kind of semi-transparent drapery. She got shakily to her feet and walked to the wall opposite her.

It was webbing. A spider's web. She touched it experimentally and recoiled at the sticky, silky feel of the web. Looking back, she saw that she had awakened on a mat made of the same stuff. Scanning the room quickly she saw a container across the room and went over to investigate. It looked like a bottle of some kind of spun glass, like hardened cotton candy. When she touched it, it was hard and smooth, and when she looked inside, what she saw made her heart leap.

Water!

Amy put the bottle to her lips and drank deeply. It tasted good. Suddenly, the webbing and the rock wall of the room she was in opened and a looming shadow appeared right in front of her. Her eyes opened wide in surprise and she began to choke on the mouthful of water, coughing and spitting it out at the same time.

Elmo wiped the water out of his eyes. "Hey, watch what you're doing, why don't you!" he said angrily.

But Amy didn't even notice him. Behind him stood one of the Great Spiders, the huge black arachnoids that had made a prisoner of Earth and everyone on it. She could see where a few glistening drops of water clung to its body as it backed up, pumping up and down and swiping at the wet spots with a spike-like front leg.

"Elmo, watch out!" Amy yelled, backing away from her friend and the horrible spider behind him.

Elmo smiled. "Don't worry about him, he's friendly," he told her. "At least for now. He's just mad because you got him a little wet, that's all. They really do have something about water here. I haven't seen a drop of the stuff besides what they gave me when I woke up—and what you just spit in my face."

Amy shook her head as if she was having trouble understanding him. "Where are we? What's going on, Elmo?" she demanded.

"We are on the home planet of the spiders— it's called Drigoonaa—and we are about to go to court," Elmo told her.

Amy could only blink as Elmo and the spider led her out of the room.

They walked through glistening hallways of spun webbing and light and rock. Spiders, mostly the ones they had met already in the cave back on Earth, the small mottled ones, scuttled around them on business of their own. Some of the great black ones were there as well, huge and dangerous-looking.

As they walked through caverns and along

gleaming, gauzy hallways filled with soft vibrating light, Elmo explained what he had found out while Amy had been sleeping off the effects of their trip.

"I'm still not sure how we got here. It has something to do with their Web/Mind thingy. This guy"—Elmo pointed ahead at the Great Spider leading the way—"this guy is some kind of guard. And..."

Elmo stopped talking as suddenly the Great Spider halted at a wall of bare rock, again covered by glistening web, and the wall opened.

Enter, a voice boomed.

Amy and Elmo looked at each other. The Great Spider went ahead into the chamber beyond, and after a few seconds' hesitation, the kids followed.

They found themselves in a huge cavern. Ranged in a large circle in the center of the cavern, seven spiders, the smaller, mottled ones, sat with their legs tucked under them on short pillars made of web. Above their heads, an umbrella of flashing light and buzzing electricity floated in the air, every once in a while touching one of the seven and spreading over their bodies so that they glowed with a green-gold luminescence.

Then the voice began.

We are Kramath. We are the ancient rulers of Drigoonaa and the progenitors of the great Web/Mind.

"What do you want with us?" Amy demanded, stepping forward.

We are Kramath.

"You said that already," Elmo shot at whoever was speaking.

Silence! You are rebels. We know you are fighting our kind on your planet. We know where your forces are and we know that they will be defeated.

Amy and Elmo looked at each other. There was nothing left to say.

CHAPTER 2

MUDDY WATER

"What do you think they're waiting for?" Earl asked, glancing around the marsh nervously.

Johnny and Earl knew that their plane must have been spotted, because they had crash-landed in the swamp. So far, though, they had seen nothing but swamp grass, mosquitoes, and a few tadpoles.

Johnny stood beside his friend, knee-deep in mud. He pulled one foot out of the muck with a sucking noise accompanied by the smell of rotten eggs as swamp gas was released into the air.

"Maybe they're waiting for the smell to kill us," Johnny offered, wrinkling his nose.

"Well, if your flying didn't do it, nothing will," Earl told him.

"Hey, I would've liked to see you do any better, dude!" Johnny answered testily.

"I never said I could fly," Earl countered.

"Well, I never said I could land," Johnny retorted.

"You might've said something about that *before* takeoff," Earl told him.

"Oh, what was I supposed to say? Sorry, but we're going to be spider bait because even though we might escape, I never learned how to land a plane?" Johnny demanded sarcastically, splashing Earl with black swamp water.

Earl looked shocked as the mucky water ran down his face. "Don't splash me," he said ominously, blinking mud out of his eyes.

He threw a handful of muck and water at Johnny suddenly, laughing out loud. For a moment they forgot how much trouble they were in. They played as they might have if the world weren't the way it was.

Unfortunately, it was—and they were in a lot of trouble.

Giant spiders ruled the Earth, and Johnny and Earl had been on a desperate flight, in perhaps one of the last airplanes on the planet, to reach a rebel base known only vaguely as Avalon.

"Wait a minute," Johnny shouted. "We don't have time to play, man. Those creepy-crawlers could be here any second. We have to figure something out," he reminded his friend, his face a stern mask.

The boys looked at each other unsmilingly. Earl turned to survey the swamp. They had chosen it because everyone knew that the Great Spiders didn't like water. Whether that applied to swamp water, they really didn't know, but it had been worth a shot. The plane had sunk into the water and soft mud almost immediately. Johnny and Earl had just had time to get out, bruised and shaken but otherwise okay.

"Hey, Earl, I think I have a plan," Johnny announced, snapping his fingers. "The sun's going down. It'll be dark soon."

"Yep, the sun is rising and setting—thanks for the info," Earl responded sarcastically.

"What I mean is, I say we get away from here a little ways, and then hide out until it's dark," Johnny said.

Earl shaded his eyes and looked at the sun. It was a reddening ball falling in the west. "I guess the least we could do is get away from here. Then after that..." Earl began.

Johnny nodded. "Yeah, after that..." Johnny couldn't finish either. Neither of them wanted to say what they would do "after that," because neither of them knew.

Johnny nodded. They looked at each other and started forward, sloshing through the muck without saying anything. When they were about a hundred yards away from where the plane went down, Earl turned to Johnny and said, "I guess when you are being chased by giant spiders, it's way better to know how to take off than it is to know how to land."

Johnny laughed and clapped his friend on the back. "You know, landing's pretty important, too," he responded.

The two boys started forward again, heading into the setting sun.

"Oh, man, spider central!" Earl gasped as he gazed in front of him.

The marshland they had been traveling through ended here. As they walked farther from the wreckage, the small grassy islands eventually disappeared. Likewise, the many oily streams they had been following had eventually combined into one large stream, leading the wet, exhausted boys into a concrete flood control channel. There, the water began to move quickly as it disappeared into a tunnel with a watery roar.

On one side of the tunnel were open fields. It looked as though some kind of housing tract had once occupied the site. All that was left now, however, were only the charred, moonlit remains of houses.

And on the other side of the channel—were the spiders!

The spider base, or whatever it was, consisted of some large barracks-like buildings and little else. Above the buildings and surrounding them on all sides were the webs spun by the new masters of the Earth.

The boys ducked down. A truck, gears grinding, drove into the compound, followed by another and then another. Ten trucks in all arrived in the compound and, as if on cue, people got out of the backs of the trucks and formed neat lines on the blacktop pavement.

However, they were not people: they were the webbed ones—the conquered humans forced to serve the will of the Great Spiders. The people were silent. Wearing identical black coveralls, each of them had the web implants on their faces.

"It must be a base for the webbed ones," Earl whispered.

"Man, I wish I had a couple of hand grenades right about now," Johnny whispered back.

The boys slid down the concrete slope a little. The boys looked at each other, then Johnny nodded. "Wait here a minute," he said as he slid down toward the bottom of the channel.

From his new vantage point, Johnny looked

into the roaring inky blackness of the tunnel, wondering where it went. It was a good bet that the tunnel went all the way to the ocean. The Pacific couldn't be far. The question was, if the water emptied into the ocean, would it take Earl and Johnny with it?

"Hey, Earl," Johnny hissed, looking back up toward his friend. Then his heart almost stopped. Earl was poised to leap over the embankment.

What was he doing?

CHAPTER 3

TAKING SIDES

"We're not rebels. We're patriots. The Earth is our planet, and we are just fighting for what is ours!" Elmo yelled at the top of his lungs, spinning around and glaring at the circle of Kramath.

The umbrella of light flickered ominously above their heads for a moment. Amy reached out and pulled Elmo closer to her. "I hope you didn't overdo it," she told him.

That is good. We are patriots, too, the voice said.

Elmo and Amy glanced at each other. "What do you mean?" Elmo asked.

We are also fighting for what is ours.

"The Earth is not yours!" Amy responded.

Not Earth. Drigoonaa.

"What?" Amy and Elmo said at the same time.

We are Kramath. In your language it means *Those who think*.

"I bet you can't tell what I'm thinking right this minute," Elmo mumbled under his breath. Amy nudged him in the ribs to shut him up, and the voice continued.

**The ones against whom you fight for the survival of your planet are Grralath, *the ones who do*.

**Eons ago, before your race existed, Kramath and Grralath were one people. We had an empire that stretched among the stars and was held together by the power of the Web/Mind. Grralath were the workers and Kramath were the thinkers and we lived together.

There were those among the Kramath who were proud. They saw the Grralath as lesser creatures and toyed with their bodies and their minds until the Grralath were forced to save themselves by force. They turned against those who think and sought to destroy us.

"Sounds like they had a pretty good reason," Elmo muttered.

The voice continued without commenting on Elmo's statement.

They sought to destroy us, but my kind found refuge underground. We have lived under the surface of Drigoonaa for longer than your race has existed. We now wish to return to what is ours.

"So let me get this straight," Amy started. "You guys are fighting the same big spiders, like this one," she motioned at one Grralath spider, standing nearby, "and you brought us here to tell us that?"

We have a few allies among the Grralath. Even now, there are those who seek the old wisdom. We brought you here to make you understand.

"Understand what? Sounds to me like you guys made your own bed—now you can lie in it!" Elmo said sneeringly.

**As I said, we were proud, but we have learned in our long exile. We wish to rejoin our brothers the Grralath and make Drigoonaa what it once was.

We have knowledge that the Grralath lack. Our understanding of the Web/Mind could make them a whole people again. One with us. Without that knowledge, they will continue to sink into barbarism, and Drigoonaa will never be whole again.

"It sounds to me like this is just a big excuse for you guys to take over and force the Grralath —that's what you called them, right?—to play second fiddle again," Elmo said.

You have seen what they are doing to your Earth.

Neither Amy nor Elmo responded. It wasn't a question. It was a simple statement of fact.

Your planet is the first in a string of conquests planned by the Grralath. When they destroyed our power, they also destroyed the power of the Web/Mind, which they do not really understand. It has taken them eons to begin to reestablish the empire, but they have finally begun.

"Reestablish the empire?" Amy asked.

That is their plan.

"And you are trying to tell us that you guys would do something different?" Elmo asked.

We are no longer interested in empire. We Kramath are interested in peace and reunification of our people. Nothing more.

"And you can do this with this Web/Mind?" Amy asked.

Yes.

"So go ahead and do it. We don't mind—" Amy began, when all at once the umbrella of light over the spiders' heads began to shoot brightly colored sparks that curled and flamed around the room.

At that moment a jumble of sounds—voices, Amy thought—filled the air and the Kramath, who until that time had remained perfectly still, leaped from their places and began to converge on Amy and Elmo.

"What is going on?" Amy yelled.

A din of voices coursed through the air, totally incomprehensible to Amy and Elmo, who now found themselves surrounded once again by agitated-looking giant spiders. Suddenly, above the clamor, a voice speaking English, but barely understandable, focused on them.

**We are under attack. We did not expect this.

You must come with us.

CHAPTER 4

DOWN THE HATCH

"Earl!" Johnny shouted hoarsely, running back up the embankment. He made it to the top just in time to see Earl sail over the safety rails and start walking toward the compound. Johnny went after him at full speed. Catching up to him, he grabbed Earl by the arm, spinning him around.

"What are you doing? C'mon, we have to get out of here!"

Earl looked at Johnny for a split second and then wrenched himself away violently from his friend. "I can't go. I have to do something," Earl said stiffly, turning back toward the web-covered compound. "My folks, Johnny—my parents are in there. I saw them."

Johnny's eyes opened wide. "Are you sure?" he asked.

"Yes," Earl said quickly, and started once again toward the compound.

"Earl, we have to get out of here! You can't help your parents by getting caught. You'll just be turned into one of them!" Johnny began, but his words were cut off by a number of terrifying outlines scuttling down the web that covered the base. The spiders had seen them! The spiders were coming! At that moment a voice, artificially amplified, reached them through a background of revving engines.

"Stop where you are. Stop and hold!" the voice told them. It was coming from a webbed one driving a Jeep down the service road that ran along the flood-control channel.

Earl squared his shoulders and planted his feet a little ways apart, as Johnny had seen him do when he had gotten into fights back in Blue Water. Johnny tugged at him as the spiders reached the ground. He pulled Earl to the embankment and shoved him over the rail. Earl found his feet and looked at Johnny.

"Into the water—go!" Johnny shouted, jumping over the rail and bounding down the embankment. The two of them raced down the concrete incline and hit the water at the same time, just as the spotlight from the Jeep hit the mouth of the tunnel. As Johnny and Earl entered the total blackness of the tunnel, Johnny heard the voice of the webbed one in the Jeep.

"Stop and hold, you cannot escape. In the name of the..."

All at once, Johnny was swallowed by darkness and all he could hear was the roar of the water and the beating of his heart.

The walls of the tunnel were slick with algae, and Johnny slid off them as the water bounced him from one side of the conduit to the other. He got his breath when he could, gasping for air before he was pulled under by the swirling currents in the narrow tube. He couldn't see anything: the inside of the tunnel was the pitchest black he had ever experienced. Both senses of seeing and hearing were useless in the darkness and roar of the drainage tunnel.

All he could do was keep himself balled up as tightly as possible and ride out the push of the water as it made its way, he hoped, to the sea. He had lost track of Earl right after they had entered the tunnel mouth. They had tried to link arms, but the current was too strong. The last he had felt of his best friend was the touch of his fingers as they had slipped from around his wrist and vanished.

At a certain point, Johnny could feel the rush of the water taking on new force. The time in between careening from one side of the conduit to the other became less and less, and he realized that the tunnel was narrowing, the water flowing even more quickly as its course was constricted. As he thought about what this meant, he felt himself hurled into something hard yet giving.

Something grabbed at his face. Johnny tried to scream but ended up swallowing a mouthful of water instead. Again he felt the wet touch of something horrible brush across his face and grab at his body.

He tried to rise to the surface of the water but found that he didn't know which way was up or down. He was being tumbled around like clothes in a washing machine when he bumped once more into whatever slimy, tentacled thing was barring his way—and he was free.

He flew out of the tunnel and into an open space, pulling in great, deep lungfuls of air. He seemed to sail through a black nothingness and then he hit the water again, sinking down and down until he finally felt the bottom of the horrible pit the current had dragged him to. He pushed up, flailing with his arms and legs toward a surface he couldn't see but only sensed. At last, his head broke the water, and he breathed.

"Johnny, Johnny, Johnny, Johnny!" His name echoed through the chamber. It was Earl's voice.

"Earl!" he answered, listening to the echoes of his own voice as he treaded water. Wherever they had ended up, the current no longer pulled at him—and Earl was there and alive.

Johnny told Earl to keep calling his name, and eventually he found his friend.

"Johnny, we made it," Earl said.

"Just barely—something attacked me right before I spilled into this place—whatever this place is," Johnny told him, peering into the midnight black, trying to make out his friend's face.

"Oh, man, me too. It had these slimy fingers and these really big teeth and..." Earl said.

Johnny laughed. "Dude, that must've been me. We must've run into each other."

Earl laughed then, too. "Well, in that case it was even uglier than I thought," he said.

"Very funny," Johnny replied.

That's when the first hand grabbed him. He felt it close over his mouth and pull him down. Suddenly, he was underwater, struggling in the grip of something he couldn't see. Whatever it was, there were more than one of them, and no matter how hard he twisted and turned, he couldn't get free. The hand clamped over his mouth stayed there as he was carried out of the water and deposited on a kind of concrete shelf just above the waterline.

When the hand was finally removed, Johnny was about to yell, but the words caught in the back of his throat as a bright light shone in his eyes and a familiar voice said, "Well, it seems like I'm always having to fish you two out of the water!"

The light was taken out of his eyes and shone then on a face he knew. He couldn't believe it, but there he was.

Walter Fire-Bear.

A flare was lit then and Johnny could see in its eerie pinkish glow that Earl was beside him and that they were surrounded by men wearing scuba diving gear and carrying guns in their hands.

"Walter, what are you doing here?" Earl asked.

"I was just on my way to meet some ghosts when me and the boys heard you two caterwauling to beat the band. A better question is, what are you two doing here?" Walter asked, smiling.

One of the guys with the guns said, "These two idiots have probably compromised the operation." Then he spat, just to make sure everyone understood that he was not happy.

"Well, it seems to me that we was already compromised. We was leaving anyway, weren't we, Mitchell?" Walter answered the man.

Mitchell didn't respond.

"So, get up, boys, you might as well come with us. I imagine you're headed our way."

Johnny and Elmo looked at each other. "You're going to meet ghosts, Walter?" they asked.

Walter just smiled.

CHAPTER 5

THE TEST

"All right, that's it! I'm not going anywhere until I get some better answers than I'm getting!" Elmo said loudly.

There is no time.

"Well, you guys better make time, because I'm sick of this!" Elmo responded.

Suddenly, a huge tearing noise joined the din of sounds, and a sparking of electricity and strange fire filled the cave, lighting it with an alien glow. Then the wall through which Amy and Elmo had come when they had first entered the room opened once again, this time revealing a dangerous-looking Grralath Great Spider, gleaming black.

It scuttled into the room, stood still for a moment, and then launched itself at the nearest Kramath. The large black spider wrapped its legs around the smaller one and the two arachnoid aliens rolled across the floor of the cavern. As Amy and Elmo watched, many Kramath pounced on the battling pair and in a moment it was over.

As large and powerful as it was, the lone Great Spider was no match for the dozens of Kramath, and they brought it down like dogs tearing at a lion. It had happened in the blink of an eye, and Amy and Elmo barely heard the voice speak to them as they regarded the two dead spiders, a Kramath and the Grralath, both dead, on the floor of the Council chamber.

It is all right. He was alone. An assassin.

"What does all this have to do with us?" Amy asked breathlessly.

But the voice did not answer. Instead, the Kramath made a circle around the two bodies and a new humming noise filled the room. The umbrella of electricity condensed over the two bodies as the humming noise became louder. The Kramath and their Grralath ally stretched out their front legs, or arms, or whatever they were, and rested them on the bodies.

"What do you want from us?" Elmo yelled.

The humming noise got louder. Amy and Elmo covered their ears. The noise continued to get louder until it became an ear-piercing shriek that threatened to blow their eardrums out. And then it stopped. At the same moment, the bodies of the dead seemed to quiver. A light shone from them, then was absorbed by the umbrella of light above them, and the council chamber was quiet again.

Amy looked at Elmo. "I think that was a funeral," she told him.

We mourn our dead.

"We didn't know you did that," Elmo said.

There is much about us you do not know.

"Did you mourn for that big scary one, too?" Amy asked.

We mourn for our brother.

"I still don't see what any of this has to do with us," Amy said.

It has to do with you. Your mind is open. You can help us.

"How can I help you?" Amy asked wonderingly, looking at the spiders.

"Yeah, and why should we? We have our own problems, you know," Elmo said testily.

The voice ignored him. **Will you help us?** it asked.

"What—what can I do?" Amy responded.

Elmo hadn't thought the whole thing was a very good idea when the Kramath had first mentioned it, and looking up at Amy now, encased in webbing, seemingly floating in mid-air about three feet above the cavern floor, he was sure of it. Brilliant lights played around her, but she didn't notice them. They had told him that she would be unconscious for the first part of the trial and that then she would wake up.

"And what then?" Amy and Elmo had asked at the same time.

Then it depends on the openness of your mind and your ability to understand the messages you are sent and the things you will see, the disembodied voice had told them.

They had told the kids that before the Kramath had retreated underground at the beginning of the Grralath onslaught, they had been arrogant in their use of the Web/Mind and the sacred powers that it represented. Since their retreat, they had sworn to use it only as a tool of communication and trans- portation. However, it could still be activated as a weapon—but only through another.

And that's what Amy was for. Just because her mom had been a psychic on television, the Kramath believed that she could undergo the tests and help them activate the Web/Mind once again to its full potential.

Elmo didn't think so. But Amy did.

Around her, on the floor of the cave, the Kramath of the Council were once again arranged in a circle. They had told him that if he interfered in any way during the ritual, the Web/Mind would not be activated and Drigoonaa and the Earth would probably be doomed.

Elmo kicked listlessly at the ground. So far, there hadn't been much to see. Amy slept in her cocoon of alien spider web while the Council filled the cavern with a low keening noise like the sound of wind through trees.

What are trees?

Elmo spun around at the sound of the voice in his head. A Kramath had come to stand beside him and had laid one of its legs on his head so lightly that he hadn't even noticed it.

"Back off, spider face," Elmo growled at the Kramath.

The Kramath did not remove its leg. Instead, Elmo heard, **I am Talu.**

Elmo blinked. Was that its name?

In her cocoon of spider webbing, Amy stirred. Elmo saw her move her head. She said something, but he couldn't hear what it was.

Your friend is good. I am Talu.

"Your name is Talu?" Elmo asked the Kramath, without taking his eyes off Amy.

Talu. You are Elmo? We are young ones together, the Kramath told Elmo. He, or it, seemed to be trying to make friends with Elmo.

"How come you have to touch me to talk but the other ones don't?" Elmo asked.

Only the council speaks with the voice of the council. You are human.

"Duh," Elmo responded sarcastically. Then he saw Amy move again. Her eyes opened and she smiled. Elmo couldn't tell if she was smiling at him, but she seemed to be all right. The noise in the cavern grew in intensity, and the lights flashing around Amy began to blink—red, gold green, gold red...

I have never seen human before. Other human on Drigoonaa is not available to us, Talu said.

"Well, I've seen enough of you guys to last a lifetime," Elmo responded, still watching Amy closely. Then he realized what the outer space spider had said, and he turned to face it.

"Other human?" he asked.

Prisoner of Grralath. I have heard of. You are very ugly.

"Oh, yeah? Well—" Elmo began. Then he decided to ignore it. "What do you mean, prisoner?"

Human prisoner. I have heard...

Amy screamed.

Elmo spun around to see what was happening, and the first thing he noticed was that the circle of spiders had moved closer and that the floating, blinking lights were concentrating on Amy's head.

Before he and Amy had been led to separate rooms so that she could be prepared for the ritual, he had been told that he couldn't interfere. They had said they wouldn't hurt her.

She screamed, her eyes wide with fright or pain.

Elmo took a step toward her.

Friend all right, Talu's voice said in his head. Then Elmo took another step and broke contact. Amy was now shivering, her face contorted into a mask of pain. If he interfered, they had told him, the ritual would be polluted—the Web/Mind would not activate to its fullest potentiality—whatever that meant. Amy groaned and the spiders scuttled nearer her. Her whole head seemed to be encased in a helmet of different colored lights, which were now spinning faster and faster.

"Johnny, Mom, Earl!" Amy called out.

Elmo didn't know what do. If he tried to stop it, it might mean the end of the Earth. The Kramath had explained the power of the Web/Mind and also what it could do. But Amy was in pain!

"Elmo!" Amy called out.

That was it! Elmo ran between the Council Kramath, expecting to be stopped at any moment. All he could see was Amy, bound and covered now from head to toe in flashing, pulsating lights. Her head was rocking back and forth. She seemed to be struggling to get out of the webbing. Elmo dodged between two Council Kramath, but no spiky leg shot out to bring him down. He made it to the center of the circle formed by the Kramath and reached out for his friend, turning to the Council at the same time.

"That's enough!" he yelled. He touched the webbing in which Amy was encased and she drifted softly to the floor of the chamber, while the lights that had been flashing around her and covering her with their alien glow dispersed to fill the whole cavern. The Kramath, at the same time, began to converge on Elmo, tightening their circle and blocking everything from view except for their legs and bodies, lit by the alien lights.

Suddenly, Amy disappeared. "Man, I've really done it now," Elmo thought.

"Elmo!" It was Amy. She walked toward him between the bodies of the Council Kramath with a big smile on her face.

"What's going on? What are you doing there? You were just here," Elmo demanded, waving his arms at the place on the ground where Amy—or whatever it was—had disappeared.

"I'm sorry, Elmo, it was a test. A test for all of us."

"But what about the Web/Mind? What about..."

Amy cut him off. "They wanted to see if you would help me, even though they warned you that you would blow it big time if you did. They were testing us. What you saw was a projection of me. They were testing us all, and we passed," she told him. Then she turned to the nearest Kramath. "We did pass, didn't we?"

You passed. The Web/Mind can now be activated to its full potential. To protect ourselves, we must also use it to protect another worthy species. You are found worthy, the voice told her.

Then suddenly, the lights that filled the cavern coalesced into a shining Web over their heads. **You must bring a message to your people,** the voice said.

Amy and Elmo nodded and listened as the Kramath gave them a message for the people of Earth.

CHAPTER 6

GHOSTS

"So how long do we sit here, Walter?" Joe, one of Walter's men, asked as Johnny and Earl and Walter and his men crouched in the darkness of an old movie theater somewhere in what used to be downtown L.A.

Walter and his men—Walter's Warriors, they called themselves—were looking for the Ghosts, a group of rebels who had been operating undercover in Los Angeles since the Great Spiders had consolidated their control over Southern California.

Walter had explained earlier that they had made a rendezvous to meet the Ghosts in the movie theater because they had some important information for Avalon Base. "Well, I guess we'll sit here a while longer," Walter answered him.

"They're not coming," Joe complained.

"What was that?" A crashing sound came

from somewhere in the dark theater. A flash-
light beam cut through the gloom and glinted
off the beady red eyes of a rat rummaging
through some boxes.

"Oh, it's just a rat," one of the men said,
relieved.

"It looks like we have a whole bunch of rats
here," a voice in the darkness hissed.

There was a scuffling sound, then a light
went on. They were surrounded by webbed
ones! Walter, Johnny, Earl, and the rest jumped
to their feet. They were caught!

"Nobody move," one of the webbed ones said.
The webbed ones seemed unarmed, except for
the mean-looking clubs that they held at the
ready. The one who was speaking tapped his
club menacingly on his outstretched palm.

Walter's group backed together, facing out-
ward, peering at the webbed ones. They waited
for the webbed ones to make the first move.

"You must be Walter's Warriors," another
voice said.

Earl looked up when he heard that voice. It
was a voice he knew. He barely dared to look—
and then he saw them.

He broke formation. Walter yelled at him to
stop. The webbed ones came at him with their
clubs up, ready to smash him down. Earl didn't
stop. He raised his hands to ward off the clubs.

Then a woman standing behind them said, "Stop it, let him pass." Her soft voice didn't seem as if it could come from a slave of the spiders.

All at once, Earl was hugging the woman, and he was being patted on the back and hugged by a man who had joined them.

All Earl could say was "Mom, Dad—you're alive. You're alive!"

"But why can't you?" Earl demanded. "It's safe back on the island!"

Mrs. Two-Sticks shook her head slowly, her long black hair tied back in a ponytail. Her dark eyes looked affectionately and sadly into the eyes of her son. "We can't, Earl. We still have work to do here. We'll be all right. It's so good to see you, son." She hugged him close to her and then held him out at arm's length. "I thought I might never see you again," she finished.

"I never thought that—never," Earl told her.

"Your mother is right, Earl," Mr. Two-Sticks told him, laying a large, powerful hand on his son's shoulder. "We have to stay here and continue to gather intelligence. There's something going on and we're not sure what it is yet. You go back to the island with Walter. We'll see each other again when all of these hairy monsters are dead, if not before," he assured Earl.

Just then, Walter called out, "We have to get going. We have to rendezvous with the boat."

Mr. Two-Sticks turned from Earl and addressed Walter and the rest of Walter's Warriors. "All right, now you've met the Ghosts. Walter, it's good to see you again, but there's business to take care of. We have something for you to tell your commanders back at Avalon Base. There is something big going on.

"The creepy-crawlers are using the webbed ones to build something huge, some giant machine. We don't know what it is yet or what it's for, but the spiders seem to be converging here from all over the place. More and more are gathering every day around the Coliseum. We've only glanced at what they're doing, but it's big, whatever it is," Mr. Two-Sticks finished.

"And what about the people here. Why do they seem so—I don't know—so lifeless?" Earl asked his mom.

Mrs. Two-Sticks frowned. "All we can figure out is that the spiders are turning up the power on the control webs, however they do that. That's how they are forcing the people to work on their machine," she explained.

Everyone was silent for a moment. That's when the webbed one found them. They hadn't seen him come in.

"What are you—who are you? I will call the masters. I cannot read you," the man said. He stood unsteadily, weaving back and forth as if he was about to collapse. His speech was slurred and there was a ribbon of drool coming out one side of his mouth.

Mrs. Two-Sticks grabbed Earl and hugged him close again for just a second. Suddenly, the lights went out. Seizing the opportunity, Walter hit the webbed one on the back of the head with a solid crunching sound that left the poor slave of the spiders a crumpled mass on the ground.

Walter's voice sounded in the darkness. "Gee whiz, I guess I don't know my own strength," he said. "Well, I reckon it's time to get going," he added after a moment, and Johnny, Earl, and Walter's Warriors all moved out with Walter in the lead.

Mr. and Mrs. Two-Sticks were already gone. That's why they called them the Ghosts.

They made it back to the beach without any mishaps by staying on the back streets and imitating the half-dead walk of the webbed ones. When they were gathered on the shore, they flattened their bodies against the damp sand, waiting for the one faint flash of light that would tell them that a boat was out there waiting for them. While they waited, Earl crawled over to Johnny and whispered, "My parents are alive, they're alive! They're the Ghosts!"

"I know, Earl. That's great," Johnny responded.

Earl thought for a minute and then said, "We'll find your dad, Johnny. I know it."

"Yeah, I know," Johnny said, shrugging it off. "I wonder where the boat is?"

"There," Walter said happily. "There's the light! There's Holloway!"

They all looked out at the water. There was a light, but it didn't look like any light they had ever seen.

"What're they doing?" Walter asked in a hushed voice.

Then the light started moving toward them. It came at them faster and faster, a glowing red-orange ball!

"That's not ours," Walter muttered. "I don't know what that is."

The ball kept advancing until it was within ten feet of Walter's Warriors. It cast a reddish glow over their faces.

Greenish bolts of electric fire shot suddenly from the ball. Dancing over and around Walter's Warriors, the light encircled them and formed a Web over them that crackled and hummed with a secret, otherworldly power.

"We're dead," Earl whispered. "Bye, Mom and Dad."

"Bye, Earl," Johnny said. "It was nice knowing you."

At that moment they heard the sound of an outboard motor. Johnny thought for a moment that they were saved. The motor had to be a boat from Avalon Base coming for Walter's Warriors, he thought joyously.

That's when the spiders appeared. They seemed to materialize out of nowhere. Walter's Warriors were surrounded!

CHAPTER 7

REUNION

"Walter!" a voice cried out.

"Over here, Major Holloway," Walter answered.

A moment later, Major Holloway, a grizzled, bearded career officer, leaped into the circle of light cast by the glowing Web floating over their heads. He peered around at the spiders ringing them in.

"What's going on here, Walter?" he asked the old man.

"I wish I knew, Major, I really wish I did," Walter replied.

Major Holloway put his hand on the butt of the pistol that he wore under his shoulder.

Suddenly the spiders scuttled forward, closing the gap between themselves and the humans facing them. Major Holloway clicked the safety off on his pistol and pulled it halfway out of its holster.

"I know bullets don't do any good against you creepy-crawlers," murmured the major, "but a little noise would make me feel a whole lot better right about now."

At that moment, there was another jostling among the spiders, and the major pulled his pistol out and pointed it up in the air.

But he didn't fire.

The spiders weren't advancing—they were spreading out, clearing a way through the mass of their clustered bodies to reveal two humans.

"Amy!" Johnny shouted, rushing forward. "Elmo!"

The four friends met in the midst of the spiders. Amy hugged Johnny and Earl, and Elmo got a punch in the arm from Johnny. Then Earl grabbed Elmo in a headlock and gave him a super-noogie.

"Where have you guys been?" Earl asked, still holding Elmo in an affectionate headlock.

"We were getting instructions from the Kramath!" Elmo said, his voice muffled by Earl's armpit.

"The what?" Johnny asked.

"The Kramath—these spiders. The others are called Grralath, the Great Ones—Johnny, Earl, we have so much to tell you!" Amy said excitedly.

"Let me go, Earl, you dork!" Elmo demanded.

Earl grinned and released Elmo from the headlock. "That's the Elmo I know," he said.

Major Holloway stepped up to them. He smiled and then looked around suspiciously. "These spider friends of yours—can you tell me what they want exactly?" the major asked Amy.

"They need us all to fall back to Avalon. They can't keep up the Web/Mind for very long, and they—well, maybe I'd better let them tell you," she finished mysteriously.

The Kramath around them shuffled forward.

"Don't worry about it, Major Holloway," said Johnny. "Amy's mom used to be a psychic on TV. If she says it's all right—it's all right."

"It *is* all right—isn't it, Amy?" Earl asked her, glancing at the spiders as they raised their front legs in unison, thrusting them into the air like spikes.

Amy shrugged. "Well, it is, and it isn't," she said.

And the spikes came down, landing gently on the human heads.

The major stood for a moment with a weird look on his face. Then the Kramath released him and the others they were touching. The humans staggered back, looking confused.

The major shook his head, then glared at the

spiders and at Amy and Elmo. "How do I know this isn't some kind of trap? We must be lighting up this beach for miles," he said suspiciously.

Amy cleared her throat. "Don't worry, Major, nobody, er, nothing—no spiders or anything—can see us, at least right now. We're protected by the Web/Mind," she explained. "That's the weird thing." She pointed at the flashing Web of light above them.

Then Elmo stepped forward. "Yeah, but they can't keep it up for long. We have to get out of here. I just asked them if we could find you first, and they sure did," he finished.

"You asked them if they could find *us?*" Earl asked incredulously.

"You know it, man. I mean I hate you, and you hate me, and everything. But I still wanted to make sure you guys were all right. You need me, you know?" Elmo said, smiling.

Earl grabbed him and gave him another big noogie. "And you need some more of these," he said.

Then Amy said, "We have to move. The Kramath told us about a base nearby, a rebel base."

"Yeah, that's Avalon Base," the major informed them.

The rest of Walter's Warriors crowded

around as Johnny asked, "What are they doing? I mean, what's going on?"

"I'll tell you everything. I mean, Elmo and I will. We've been...It's so complicated, but these spiders—they call themselves the Kramath—they're allies. They're revolting," Amy said breathlessly.

"They sure are," Earl threw in.

"Very funny, Earl. No, they're revolting on their own planet. Elmo and I have been up there and—"

The Kramath nearest Amy shot out its arm and touched her head. Amy nodded, and the spiky appendage was withdrawn.

"We have to go. The Kramath will take us to Avalon Base in this ship," Amy said.

"I don't see any ship," one of Walter's Warriors said.

"It's a ship, kind of. I can't explain right now—"

"All right! If you can get us to Avalon Base—I say let's get out of here," Walter said.

A moment later, the ball of orange-red light had appeared again and flown away from the beach with the rebels on board. The next morning, the only thing left to prove they had been there at all was an inflatable boat drifting offshore and a muddle of human and Kramath footprints in the sand.

CHAPTER 8

HIGH AND DRY

"This machine that they're building, the one that Earl said that his parents saw, it's a kind of dehydrator. The Grralath are going to dry up the Earth to make it like Drigoonaa—and they're going to start in two days," Amy told Major Holloway.

The major stared at the young girl in utter disbelief. She stopped talking for a moment, probably to let the news she sink in.

"So you're telling me these, Kram—Kram—" he stuttered.

"The Kramath. It means 'those who think,'" Elmo informed him self-importantly.

"Right," Major Holloway said, nodding. "These Kramath creepy-crawlers want to help us? And you've been to their planet?"

"Yes, sir," Amy told him. "They want to help us, and they want *us* to help them."

Major Holloway nodded again and stroked

his beard. Then he walked to the wall to examine a map of the world pinned there. The map had five red circles on it. One of the circles encompassed Catalina Island, and the other four circled similar islands where rebel bases were either known—or thought—to exist.

Not much against a world full of spiders, Holloway mused. Then he turned back to the kids. *They're just kids!* he almost said out loud.

"And you expect me to believe this?" Holloway asked them point-blank.

"You have to believe it because it's true. The Grralath, the ones we are fighting, are here to begin rebuilding their empire, the old Empire of Drigoonaa. They're starting with Earth!" Amy said, becoming frustrated.

Elmo stepped forward. "Major Holloway, you have to believe us. We have two days. The Kramath are powering up their Web/Mind to retake Drigoonaa—"

"What is this Web/Mind, anyway?" Major Holloway interrupted.

Johnny stepped forward at this point. Major Holloway liked Johnny. He had known the kid's father, Major Coombs, and he liked Johnny's serious mind. The kid would have made a good officer one day, Holloway thought. Too bad he would probably never get the chance.

"Major Holloway, sir. I don't know what this Web/Mind is, but I've seen what it can do. If Amy says it will help, I think we have to believe her," Johnny told the major.

"It's some kind of weapon," Elmo interjected. "They need a couple of days to power it up to full potentiality. They want us to hit the beach at the same time that they start their offensive on Drigoonaa—"

"Hit the beach with what, young man?" Major Holloway demanded suddenly.

This had been the problem since the first spiders had appeared. Nothing seemed to harm them. Bullets had bounced right off of them—those bullets that had been fired, anyway. The spider takeover had happened so quickly and was so unexpected that entire armies had gone down before the advancing arachnoids. No government on Earth had wanted to launch a nuclear strike against the invaders—and soon there weren't any governments left, as far as anyone knew. There were just rebels, fighting against an enemy that seemed to be unbeatable.

"With water," Amy said quietly.

"With *what?*" Major Holloway asked.

"With water. You know—plain old, everyday, garden-variety tap water. Seawater, which we have plenty of, is even better," Elmo told him.

"Attack spiders with water?" Johnny asked.

"Yeah," Amy said. "Everybody knows they don't like it. When we were up on Drigoonaa, we found out why. There is no water there, not a drop. They don't need it, and more than that, it can hurt them!"

"But we've seen them, Amy. Johnny and I saw them in the rain and we've all seen them getting wet," Earl said for everybody.

"Oh, they can stand a little of it, especially cold water, but—"

"This is ridiculous!" Major Holloway said suddenly. "You kids come in here with this crazy story about flying around to other planets and good spiders and everything else, and now you want me to believe that we can fight these creepy-crawlers with water? This is just too much!"

At that moment the lights went dead and a low rumbling shook the floor under his feet.

"What is going on now?" Holloway demanded.

Amy's voice was barely a whisper. "They're using the Web/Mind," she said.

"What, Amy? What did you say?" Johnny asked.

"Will somebody please tell me what's going

on here?" Major Holloway demanded as the auxiliary power brought on the yellow emergency lighting.

"Something is using the Web/Mind, Major Holloway," Amy explained. "Something that doesn't know how to use it very well, and that something is going to pay us a visit," she added.

Outside, the sun was shining in a bright cloudless sky. A soft breeze was blowing, bending the short grass that grew on most of the island. Here and there were clumps of oak trees, and in the distance, a herd of American bison grazed peacefully. There had been a herd of bison on Catalina for a long time. The rebels of Avalon Base felt a special relationship to the lumbering, powerful beasts; they were perhaps the last of their kind, whether the bison knew it or not.

Johnny, Earl, Amy, and Elmo, along with Major Holloway and some of his underofficers, looked through the slitted windows of an observation box buried in the side of a small, natural-looking but man-made hill. Another officer joined them and whispered something to Major Holloway. The major nodded and dismissed the man.

"What did you say was going to happen, little girl?" one of the major's aides asked Amy as she peered out at the seemingly peaceful day.

"Well, mister," she began in a sarcastic tone. "What I think is going to happen is that a bunch of nasty spiders are going to come and crunch your head into little tiny pieces."

Johnny slapped his forehead and grimaced. It was hard to believe some of the things that came out of Amy's mouth sometimes. That girl wasn't afraid of anything. The junior officer looked startled for a moment and then laughed. He looked at his fellow officers and said, "Isn't she cute?" The other officers started to laugh.

Suddenly, the laughter was interrupted as a huge flash of blue-green light cracked the sky.

"What the blazes was that?" Major Holloway demanded.

"They're coming," Amy said quietly.

Another flash lit the sky and then bolts radiating from a crackling kind of vortex began to shoot out in all directions. At the same time the wind began to blow harder, flattening the grass against the earth. Gradually, the bolts shooting out from the center began to take on the shape of a Web that appeared and disappeared like a fluorescent light bulb that had almost burnt out, crackling and humming in an unstable, randomly powerful way. Then suddenly, a gigantic flash shot down to the ground. The whole crackling Web structure seemed to explode and then disappear.

In its place, the huge black form of a Great Spider stood completely still on the grass.

The wind died immediately. The spider stood without moving. Johnny and the rest of them could see rebels from the base emerging from observation posts like the one they were in, moving toward the giant spider with guns drawn and at the ready.

"What are they doing?" Earl asked. "Bullets can't hurt that thing."

"Wishful thinking?" Johnny offered.

"Those guns are an experiment. They shoot a special kind of bullet," Major Holloway explained suddenly, gleefully rubbing his hands together.

"Were you expecting this?" Elmo asked.

"No, but we've been working on things, anything we can think of. As long as we have a chance to try it, we might as well. Do you think any more of these monsters are going to drop by, Amy?" Major Holloway asked.

"Oh, you believe me now?" she countered sarcastically.

Major Holloway glanced at the scene being played out on the grass outside. "I guess I have to, don't I?" he answered.

"There's something wrong with that monster," Elmo muttered.

"The Kramath said the Grralath didn't know how to use the Web/Mind properly. Maybe it got hurt transporting over," Amy suggested.

The Great Spider had to have seen or sensed its attackers by then. It didn't make any moves, though. Instead, it continued to stand still. The rebels formed a wide circle around the giant spider. A command was given—and they fired, pouring whatever new kind of bullets had been developed into the spider's gleaming black body.

The monster didn't seem to notice until the sound of the guns firing ceased at another command. It stood still for a moment longer and then it collapsed. A cheer went up from the other observation posts. Major Holloway smiled and clapped one of his officers on the shoulder. Johnny and Earl and Amy and Elmo saw rebels pouring out from their hiding places, racing toward the downed spider. The rebels who had attacked it were already examining the body at close range.

"Well, what do you know about that," Major Holloway said, clapping his hands. "We finally have something to hurt these monsters with."

One of the rebels who had fired at the monster approached it warily while the others stood back. He crept up to the prone body of the horrible arachnoid and glanced back at his friends and fellow rebels. Putting out one hand, he lightly touched one of its front legs. Then he patted it. It didn't move.

"It's okay," he yelled, turning back to face the observation posts. "It's okay, it's dead as a door—"

The leg came up like a bolt of lightning and landed on the rebel soldier's head. He started spitting and shaking immediately while the rest of the force, which had been creeping closer and closer, ran back toward the observation posts.

The unfortunate rebel caught by the giant spider continued to shake and then, slowly, his mouth started forming words. Saliva dripped from his lips as the words got louder and louder until finally the man was screaming.

"You must surrender!" he yelled. "You must surrender!"

Then the spider took him in its mandibles and the *click-click* of the giant spider's jaws was heard. The man was snipped in half like a piece of yarn, and the two halves of his body fell to the ground.

The spider regained its stance in one light-ning-like motion and seemed to be choosing another target when the ground began to tremble and the sky to darken.

"Things just keep getting better and better, don't they?" Earl asked no one in particular.

CHAPTER 9

ALLIES

The starship landed with a shuddering of many-faceted sheets of purest silver. It was hard to say what shape it was, as it reflected the sunlight pouring down on it from a thousand different angles, in turn sending light leaping in all directions. There didn't seem to be any propulsion drive. There was no exhaust.

The whole great vehicle simply settled onto the Earth. Its landing gear—great shafts of silver metal, resembling the legs of a giant spider—gouged the earth and dug in, sending a vibration up into the craft that reverberated in all parts of the gleaming machine before it finally settled and became still.

The Great Spider, interrupted in its attack on the rebels, seemed to consider the spacecraft for a moment. It couldn't look up exactly, but it took one step, and then another, away from the massive shadow of the ship. Another vibration communicated itself through the vessel.

The Great Spider underneath it stood still, its black body a deeper shadow in the shadow of the machine, and then it began to piston up and down. With another shuddering of the ship, the landing legs of the giant machine buckled and folded out and the whole thing came down with a loud squishing sound on the monster, squashing it out of existence.

In the observation post, Major Holloway turned angrily to one of his officers. "Jones, do we have any missiles left?" he demanded.

Jones, a sticky-faced guy with nervous eyes and a slouchy walk, saluted sloppily. "No, sir, Major Holloway, sir!" he barked back.

"Well, then, what are we going to do about that?" Major Holloway asked anybody who thought they had an answer. He pointed out the slitted window at the gleaming machine that had just landed right on top of Avalon Base and which, in his imagination, was filled with monstrous spiders with only one thing in mind: the total destruction of the human race. He was probably right.

"We might not have to do anything about it, sir," Johnny answered him.

"Oh, thanks a lot, kid," Major Holloway shot

back at Johnny. "We can just sit here with our—"

Johnny interrupted him, pointing out the slitted window. "Look, Major, sir."

The major looked and his eyes went wide as he caught sight of Amy approaching the spider craft.

"Get her back here!" Major Holloway cried. He turned to one of his officers and ordered him to bring the girl back.

"That's okay, we'll go get her!" Johnny answered brightly. "C'mon, Earl, Elmo, let's go save Amy!"

"Great idea. We better rescue her!" Earl agreed.

"I'm sure she knows what she's doing," Elmo said, crossing his arms over his chest.

Earl hit him on the back of the head.

"Hey, watch it!" Elmo said, spinning around and rubbing the back of his head.

"C'mon, geek-brain, let's go rescue Amy!" he told Elmo, winking.

Elmo grimaced and then gave in. "Oh, uh, oh, yeah—we better go save Amy," he said, shrugging.

The three of them ran out of the observation post and around the side of the small hill under which it was hidden. They caught up to Amy when she was still a good fifty yards from the monstrous machine. It was huge! It was still hard to tell its exact size because of the play of light over the many-angled surfaces, but it was definitely gigantic. As they drew nearer to it, the machine towered over them, blocking out the sky with a crazily tilted wall of light and angles.

"Uh, Amy, just for my own information—you know what's in there, right?" Earl asked as the four of them walked side by side, the Spider-Killers together again!

"Uh, yeah—I know what's in there," she told him.

"You hesitated. You hesitated," Earl threw in.

"I didn't!" Amy shot back as the four of them continued to walk across the grass toward the strange machine that towered over them, casting a shadow across Avalon Base.

"You did kind of hesitate, Amy. You went, 'Uh—yeah,'" Johnny said, imitating her voice.

"Well, I'm *pretty* sure what's in there—" Amy began.

"I hope it's a big can of outer space Raid!" Elmo said.

"Maybe it's a big boot with jet engines so we can crush the Great Spiders like this thing did," Earl said.

"It could be—" Johnny began, but then

stopped when a place in the gleaming metal that was near the ground started to buckle and blister. Slowly at first, and then faster, a small hole opened in the metal, its edges bubbling back as though the metal had suddenly turned liquid. The opening grew to reveal a blackness inside, an impenetrable darkness that was slowly infused with a glow that was neither dark nor light but something in between. The glow continued to grow until Johnny and Earl and Amy and Elmo began to make out the gleaming interior of the ship, at least as far as they could see. A corridor, shining metal warped and twisted into web-like designs, led away from the door into the heart of the machine.

"These, I mean, whatever's in here—they're those friends of yours, right?" Earl asked, taking a step away from the opening.

"That's what it seems like," Amy answered.

"What do you mean, seems like?" Johnny asked.

"Well, it's not like I can be a hundred percent sure. It's not like that. It's more like—"

A shape scrambled into the corridor leading away from the strange door or hatch and came shooting at them with all the speed of the Great Spiders that had claimed the Earth for their own.

"AAAAHHHHHHHH!" the Spider-Killers

screamed all at once as the shape flew at them in a tangle of legs, eye lights flashing. Then the spider was outside. It caught Elmo and knocked him down so that he lay under the spider screaming and thrashing until the alien touched his head with one of his front legs. All at once, Elmo heard a voice in his mind say, **Elmo. Talu. We are young together.**

Elmo went still. The others had already stopped screaming and approached the terrified Elmo where he lay on the ground, pinned there by the friendly Kramath.

"Talu? What are you doing here?" Elmo vaguely remembered the inquisitive, friendly— in its own way—Kramath from Drigoonaa.

"Look, Elmo's got a girlfriend," Earl teased.

Elmo scrambled to his feet. "Shut up, dorkus. It's...I met him...it...whatever...on Drigoonaa. I'm surprised he remembers me."

As they stood there talking, a number of Kramath filed out of the ship and surrounded them. Suddenly, they heard a voice seeming to come out of the air directly over their heads.

We are Council. Talu assists us.

"Who said that?" Johnny demanded, whirling around, eyeing the spiders and then looking up in the sky over their heads. He looked back at the spiders and saw that one of them was wearing a kind of box.

"That's how it was up on Drigoonaa. These guys, the Council—I guess these are the same ones—they could talk to us like normal, kind of, but all the others still have to touch you," Elmo offered.

Johnny moved forward and held out his hand. What he expected the Kramath to do with it, he wasn't exactly sure, but it seemed like a good idea at the time.

"My name is Johnny Coombs. Welcome to Earth, I guess," he said.

The Kramath reached out a leg and rested it on Johnny's head. An image of his father exploded in the boy's vision centers and left him reeling. The spider removed its appendage and Johnny shook his head to clear it.

"You know where my father is?" Johnny said to the spider.

Please show us the Council of this Web. We must transmit.

"Show us the Council of this *what?*" Earl asked.

"I think it wants us to take it to our leader," Johnny suggested.

"Oh, dude, you'd think they would try to be a little more original," Elmo said, slapping his forehead with his palm.

"But wait, what about my father?" Johnny asked.

Talu reached out a leg and touched Johnny. **Your father is with Grralath. My planet. We must win. We will have your father,** the young Kramath transmitted.

Johnny smiled. "I knew it, he's alive, alive," he said, almost whispering.

Take us to your leaders, the Kramath added, and Johnny thought, just for a second, that Talu was laughing at his own joke.

CHAPTER 10

STOWAWAYS OR CASTAWAYS?

"C'mon, man, let's get out of here," Earl urged his friend.

Johnny and Earl looked on while the Kramath directed the scientific team that had been assigned to them. It was strange to see the white-coated technicians measuring and remeasuring the liquid that the Kramath said, or transmitted, would be more effective against the Grralath. It was still water, the Kramath said; they were just rearranging the molecules a little to make it more effective. How water would help the humans against the Grralath, and why the Grralath were afraid of it, had become clear when they had taken the corpse of the smashed Grralath out from under the Kramath ship.

They were part metal! The Grralath were a race of hybrid beings—cyborg arachnoids!

**We did this to them. We wish to make

them whole again,** the Kramath had transmitted when the discovery had been made.

There was also the fact that Drigoonaa was virtually water-free. Add to this their metal parts coursing with electricity, and the reason why the Grralath were afraid of water became clear. And if the water were administered in such a way that it literally got under their skins, it could actually short-circuit them.

The Kramath didn't like water either. The lack of it on their own planet made it an unknown quantity. It seemed that it could be painful to them as well, although without the solid-state circuitry of the Grralath, it was not a real danger.

Unfortunately, despite the fact that the scientists were working well with the Kramath, who were giving them all the help they could, time was running out. All the interstellar cooperation in the universe could not make time run backward, and everyone at Avalon Base spent more and more time looking at their watches and the large clocks on the wall. They had a little less than twenty-four hours before the Grralath turned on their dehydrator and began sucking the water away from the planet. They wanted to create another Drigoonaa, and they were willing and able to destroy every living thing on Earth to accomplish their goal.

Johnny nodded. He was watching the scientists and the Kramath, but all he could think about was his father. Elmo had told him what Talu, the friendly Kramath, had told him. The rest had been filled in by the representatives of the Council Kramath. Johnny's father was indeed being held by Grralath back on Drigoonaa. He had not been webbed—the Grralath saw no need for it, since he was only one man. They used him instead to study humans. They hadn't done any permanent harm to him.

"No permanent harm!?" Johnny exploded. "What does *that* mean?"

It means that he is alive was all the Council Kramath told him.

"Let's go outside for a while," Earl said.

When they got outside, they walked automatically toward the Kramath ship. It was one of three that the Kramath said still remained. It was an incredibly old transport ship. Deploying the ball of light that was part of the Web/Mind, and in which Amy and Elmo had returned to Earth, had been the last time the Kramath had been able to use their Web/Mind powers for anything as crude as transportation.

From now until the end of the struggle that was about to take place, all the energy of the

Web/Mind had to be concentrated until it reached its full power.

As such, the Kramath had dusted off one of their ancient ships and flown it to Earth with the Council Kramath aboard. They had come to help. However, it was clear that even they were unsure whether they were in time or not.

Johnny slapped the exterior of the ship with his open palm, and the thing gave back a dull thud that did not sound like any metal Johnny had ever heard before. Then he turned to Earl.

"Earl, I have to get up there! I have to go to Drigoonaa!" he told his friend.

Earl looked at him and shrugged. He didn't know what to say.

Johnny regarded his friend, but didn't say anything either. He knew that soon the battle for both Drigoonaa and the Earth would begin. The Kramath had made it all too clear that the Grralath knew about Avalon Base and had known about it all along. They just hadn't cared about it. A handful of humans here and there on a conquered planet didn't matter much to the Grralath, as long as the planet was doomed anyway.

Johnny and Earl reached the entry hatch of the spaceship and stepped inside. The Kramath were very generous about letting the humans explore their craft. No one could really understand most of what was inside anyway. Smooth metal walls rippled and suddenly spread apart as humans or Kramath approached them. Strangely colored lights brightened and dimmed along the walls in patterns that meant nothing to humans but which Talu had explained were the ships' instructions and directories.

Boring to humans. Boring to Kramath. Boring and stupid, Talu complained one day. He was learning more words every day. **Don't do. All rules. No play like humans.**

"Well, in case you hadn't noticed, we haven't been playing much either," Earl had told the Kramath.

That is true, the Kramath had agreed.

Johnny and Earl wandered the corridors of the Kramath ship. They occasionally met with a Kramath scuttling around on some kind of errand, but mostly it seemed deserted. The two boys' footsteps echoed dully on the reflective floor as they found their way to a large chamber that seemed to be the control room for the craft. Arrayed in an arc along the wall of the ovoid chamber were a number of knobs and protrusions with lights winking above or beside them.

The knobs were designed like holsters into which the Kramath could slip their front appendages. If Johnny stuck his index finger down into one of the controls as far as he could, he could just feel the button at the bottom.

"Hey, what are you doing, trying to get us all killed?" Elmo asked, walking into the control room with Amy.

A Kramath scuttled in at that point. Completely ignoring the kids, it manipulated a few of the controls. It disappeared as quickly as it had appeared, and the kids were left alone again.

"What do you think *that* was all about?" Earl asked.

Elmo shrugged. "Beats me."

There was a new sound in the ship. The sound, like a humming, grew in intensity and then stopped abruptly. The kids looked at each other.

"These spiders are weird," Amy said.

Just then, Earl heard a voice in his head. **What are you doing?**

The boy whirled on Talu, breaking their connection. They knew him from the other Kramath by sight now. He had a distinctive bluish patch above his first right leg.

"You, you creepy-crawler! Didn't I warn you about sneaking up on me like that?" Earl raged at the Kramath.

Talu began to raise his foreleg to communicate with Earl again, but the boy slapped the spike-leg appendage away with an angry jerk of his arm.

"C'mon, Earl, he didn't mean anything. At least let him say he's sorry," Johnny urged his friend.

Earl scratched his head and glared at the spider. He was kind of cute, for an alien spider. "All right, c'mon," Earl offered, tapping himself on the head.

The weird humming shot through the ship again, and two more Kramath entered the control chamber, stationing themselves at points along the control panel. The kids watched silently as patterns of light suddenly exploded over the Kramath's positions. Three more Kramath came in and took up positions at the control board.

"Looks like they're gearing up for something," Elmo pointed out.

"Yeah. We should probably get out of here. I'm pretty hungry anyway," Johnny said.

"What?" Earl yelped suddenly, pulling back from where he had been communicating with Talu.

Johnny grabbed his friend, steadying him. "What's the matter?" he asked.

"Well, I have some good news and some bad

news," Earl announced, looking at his friends.

"What in the world are you talking about?" Elmo asked.

"C'mon with me and I'll show you," Earl told them. He led them over to where Talu was standing, next to the wall of the control center.

Earl looked at Johnny and took a deep breath.

"First the good news. It looks like we're going on a little trip," he told his friend.

Johnny and Amy and Elmo looked at him, trying to understand what he was talking about. It had something to do with what Talu had told him, but Earl wasn't giving anything away.

"Now for the bad news." Earl motioned at Talu. The metal of the wall twisted and appeared to bubble, drawing back to reveal a viewport.

Outside the ship, Catalina Island and Avalon Base were gone. They had all been replaced by a vast black emptiness dotted here and there with bright, diamond-like points of light.

"Hey, that looks like Earth," Johnny said, pointing at a blue, green, and white globe that was quickly getting smaller as they watched.

"That's the bad news," Earl told them. "We are going on a little trip to Drigoonaa."

CHAPTER 11

CRASH

"What do you mean we're on our way to Drigoonaa?" Elmo demanded.

"Take a look for yourself, dork," Earl answered him, pointing out the window at the diminishing globe of the Earth.

Johnny marched up to Talu, and the Kramath touched him.

"What is going on? Are we being kidnapped?" Johnny demanded.

There was no time. You were here. The Council could not wait. The battle for our world is beginning, Talu answered him.

Johnny backed away from Talu and gazed out the viewport. He couldn't believe it. He was going to Drigoonaa. He was going where his dad was.

"It looks like you got your wish," Amy said.

Johnny didn't say anything. He just nodded.

"Well, it wasn't *my* wish," Earl said. "I don't want to go to Drigoonaa or any other stupid planet besides Earth!" He turned to the Kramath arranged around the control boards and panels.

"Now, you turn this ship around right now or you're all dead!" Earl raged at them.

They didn't notice. Not one of the aliens turned around. Suddenly, though, a loud voice boomed out of the air above the humans.

Please allow Talu to make you comfortable in your manner. We will arrive in ten hours. Please be comfortable.

Earl looked as if he wanted to say more, but Johnny slapped him on the back, smiled, and turned to Talu. "Well, try and make us comfortable, Talu," he told the young Kramath out loud.

Talu seemed to understand him. The Kramath turned and started for a hallway, the humans following behind.

Elmo looked at Amy as they filed out of the control chamber. "You ever get the feeling that these big spiders just don't care much about us one way or the other?" he asked.

Amy gazed at the control chamber, which was filled with strange lights and controls and tools that made human technology seem like toys.

Amy smiled at Elmo. "Would you?" she asked.

An hour later they were all gathered together in the room that had been reserved for the humans aboard the Kramath vessel. The room was fashioned to resemble the rooms where both Amy and Elmo had woken up on their last trip to Drigoonaa. The walls looked like the walls of a cave, despite the fact that they shined with the gleaming, swirling patterns of the alien metal that the ship was made of. Covering the walls and hanging from the ceiling, the translucent webbing of the spider race blurred perspective and made the room seem both larger and, at the same time, smaller than it really was.

"I wonder what's going on back on Earth?" Amy asked.

"They're getting ready to spread spider guts all over the place," Earl said enthusiastically.

"I wish I was there," Amy muttered.

"Me too. I'd show those spider faces a thing or two," Elmo threw in.

"A little fresh Earth water, Mister Creepy-Crawler?" Earl said, banging his fist on the metallic floor of the ship.

"And that's all she wrote!" Elmo nodded, banging his fist on the floor in imitation of Earl. Simultaneously, the entire room lurched sickeningly to one side! All four of them were flung across the floor, landing in a tangle against one wall, enveloped in alien webbing.

"I guess I'm stronger than I thought," Elmo exclaimed when they had recovered themselves.

"I don't think that was you, Elmo," Earl whispered, wiping some of the gooey web stuff from his face.

The room lurched again, this time accompanied by a rhythmic thumping that echoed through the humans like someone playing a gigantic out-of-tune piano.

"What is going on now?" Amy asked breathlessly, glancing up at the ceiling. When she looked down again, it was just in time to see her friends scrambling through the hatch that had opened in the wall.

"Hey, wait for me!" she cried, dashing out the hatch after them.

As they entered the control chamber, another jolt shook the ship. They saw Talu at the viewport and raced over to him. Framed by the viewport, a planet rushed at them, growing larger with every second. It was strangely Earth-like, if Earth consisted almost entirely of what looked like purple desert.

"What's going on, Talu?" Elmo asked frantically, laying his hand on the Kramath's back.

The control chamber was a hive of flashing, buzzing light. The Kramath that had been guiding and running the ship were now all bathed in shifting patterns of light that skittered and blinked, giving the aliens the look of monsters from a horror movie.

We will land soon, Talu told him.

Elmo breathed a sigh of relief, glancing at the planet that was rushing at them. He told the rest of the humans what Talu had told him, and they relaxed a little.

"I hope they know more about landing than you do, Johnny," Earl said.

Johnny grimaced. Another jolt shook the ship, and the boy braced himself. "If I hear one more landing joke, I'm going to strangle somebody," he said.

There is a better word in English, Talu communicated suddenly to Elmo. **The ship is malfunctioning.**

"What better word could there be than *land?* I'd rather be just about anywhere, even on a planet full of giant spiders if I could get off this bucket of bolts," Elmo said.

A better word in your language would be crash, Talu communicated in the same calm voice he always used.

Elmo tried to say something, but the words caught in his throat. The planet Drigoonaa rushed at them through the viewport.
All Elmo could do was scream!

CHAPTER 12

DESERTED

The great purple desert stretched in all directions. A gentle wind blew the finely grained sand off the tops of dunes that marched into the distance. There, a wall of jagged mountains rose, thrusting themselves into the reddish blue sky of Drigoonaa—home world of the ancient spider masters of the universe.

About forty-five minutes after the crash landing of the Kramath vessel, Johnny rode on the back of Talu the Kramath, surveying the strange world. Up one dune and down another. It reminded him of the ocean, an ocean of purple sand that went on forever.

The crash of the Kramath vessel hadn't been as bad as it might have been. They had hurtled onto the surface of the planet, landing with a bone-crunching impact. Fortunately, no bones had actually been crunched, and when they had gotten their wits about them, the Kramath had led them outside. There, they faced a hostile and strange new world, presided over by the Great Spiders, the rulers of Drigoonaa and Earth.

The ship had been brought down in a particularly empty part of the planet. Nonetheless, the Kramath had emerged from the ship excitedly pistoning up and down. They had communicated to the humans that the offensive to retake the planet was already beginning and that they were anxious to find a Kramath outpost that they knew was nearby.

"All right, let's go kill some spiders," Earl had said.

The Kramath had told them to climb on their backs, and they started out. They moved cautiously, keeping to the bases of the dunes, climbing occasionally to the wind-blown crests to look around, and then quickly descending back into the troughs and gently sloping valleys between the mountains of purple sand. At one point they saw an army of Great Spiders in the distance. It was a long line of black, worming its way over the dunes. The humans and the Kramath had frozen then, not daring to move while the enemy column filed past.

When the Grralath were gone, the company of humans and aliens started out again. They had gone a fair distance when Johnny, doing a

bit of sightseeing with Talu, climbed carefully
to the top of a dune and spotted a glint of
something shiny in the distance.

"What's that?" Johnny had asked his spider
ally.

It is nothing.

At that moment, Johnny had formed an
image of his father, Major Coombs, in his mind.
He knew that that meant something. Talu was
not used to shielding his thoughts from the
humans. The young Kramath knew something
that he was not communicating.

"What is it?" he had demanded again.

Talu, usually so ready to talk, only communicated that they should return to the rest of the
party.

Johnny jumped off the spider's back and
began to walk toward the glint in the distance.

Talu caught up to him and tried to communicate with him, but Johnny shrugged the alien
off. He knew what the glint of shiny stuff
meant, he knew it in his heart. He had hoped
for such a long time. He picked up his pace as
he neared it. Then he broke into a run as he
drew closer to the object and began to get a
better idea of its size.

It was half buried in the purple sand, but he
knew what it was, he knew its outline by

heart. He could hear Talu scrabbling in the sand behind him, but he didn't pay any attention. He only had enough room in his mind for the large object before him. Finally, Talu forced him to descend into a trough between dunes, where he was able to touch him and communicate.

We must... the alien began.

"Why didn't you tell me? You said there was nothing out here!" Johnny demanded.

There is nothing.

"Why didn't you tell me?" Johnny demanded again, whirling around to face the spider.

I was forbidden.

Johnny broke contact and climbed as fast as he could to the top of the dune. There it was. He took a step and began to run when he lost his footing in the shifting sand and tumbled head over heels down the dune until he was brought up short against the side of the object.

It was a space shuttle. Right in front of him was the American flag and above that, the word *Marvel*. It was his father's shuttle!

Johnny got up and ran to Talu. He laid his hand on the spider's back. "Tell me where my father is," he ordered the alien.

He is near.

"Take me to him!" Johnny commanded.

The young Kramath pistoned up and down. He was getting excited. Johnny yelled at the spider-like alien. "Take me to him!"

The young Kramath went still. **All right,** it communicated finally. **May I inform the Council of our decision?**

Johnny nodded. In that instant, Johnny could sense Talu reaching out with its alien mind for the Council Kramath and communicating with them. After a moment he said, "Tell them to tell Earl and Amy and Elmo that I'll be back! I'll be back with my dad!"

A second later, the Kramath shuddered. **It is done,** it communicated.

Johnny nodded again.

Then Talu let the human climb back up on its back, and after a moment's hesitation, it scuttled and then sped up, racing away from the rest of the group, into the desert—and toward Johnny's father!

CHAPTER 13

GOING UNDERGROUND

Amy and Earl and Elmo clustered around a shining web that had appeared in the air in front of them.

"What is it?" Earl asked.

Watch, the Council voice told them.

After Johnny had disappeared and then made his announcement that he was going to find his father, they had at first tried to persuade a few of the Council Kramath to take them to their friend. The Council Kramath had refused, however, insisting that they make it to the base they were headed for as soon as possible.

The humans had almost decided to try and catch up to their friend on foot, when the whole bunch of them, Kramath and humans alike, had to hunker down into the purple sand to avoid being spotted by a lone Great Spider, skittering this way and that over the dunes.

A patrol. They are looking for us. We must hurry, the Council Kramath said.

As Amy, Earl, and Elmo watched the Great Spider search for them, methodically covering and recovering the ground in a way that made sure it missed nothing, they decided to go with the Kramath. Wherever Johnny was, he was going to be on his own for a while.

Earl didn't feel good about it, but he knew that his friend could take care of himself. So far, not even a world full of giant spiders had kept Johnny from getting where he wanted to go. A few more spiders with home-field advantage would probably just make things more interesting. That's what he hoped anyway.

It had taken them about half an hour of hard riding to reach the base. The Kramath covered the ground with a speed that made the strange sights of the spider world flash by in a blur. There were stunted bright red trees that seemed to whistle like demented trains as they passed them. They also saw some small animals that looked something like a cross between a rooster and a tricycle rolling over the sand in the distance.

The humans tried to ask questions as they sped over the sand, but they soon realized that the Kramath were either not listening or didn't care. So they grew quiet, each one thinking his or her own thoughts about what lay ahead.

Finally, they had arrived at the Kramath base, an entrance suddenly springing open in the purple sand in front of them. They had then been rushed down a labyrinth of tunnels into a large Web-coated chamber and herded to one side.

A few minutes later the shining Web appeared in front of them.

Watch.

"Watch what?" Elmo asked petulantly.

Seconds later the Web blazed to life and they saw—

"Major Holloway!?" The humans exclaimed all at once. There he was, the commander of Avalon. They could see his face. He seemed to be yelling. Then the view widened to include his arms, which were waving around wildly.

"What's happening?" Amy asked.

The Grralath are testing the dehydration device, the Council voice answered.

Then the view in the shining Web changed. They saw a huge machine surrounded by thousands of Grralath. The Great Spiders were pistoning up and down on their spiky legs as webbed ones walked listlessly among them. As the kids watched, one of the Great Spiders grabbed an unresisting human between its mighty mandibles and cut the unlucky servant in half!

"Aaahhhhhh!" Amy wailed, covering her eyes. Earl put his arms around her, but he didn't take his eyes off the Web. Another Grralath grabbed another webbed one and threw the human up into the air. The man flew high into the air and then plummeted back down to Earth, disappearing among the mighty Grralath.

"Why are they doing that? Why are they killing people for no reason?" Elmo asked, his eyes glued to the Web and the horrible images it was showing them.

They are celebrating the total defeat of their enemy. Soon they will be here.

The view in the Web changed again. This time it showed trees being blown over and bursting into flame. The view changed yet again and buildings toppled in a mighty cloud of dust and destruction.

"Is that their machine that's doing all that?" Earl asked.

Yes, the Council voice said simply.

"So what about the Web/Mind? Is it ready yet? Can't we stop them?" Earl asked anxiously.

**No. The Web/Mind is not ready. Soon. Soon

enough to save Drigoonaa? We do not know. Soon enough to save the Earth? We do not know. The Grralath will soon be here.**

"Is there any way to stop them?" Earl asked again.

We must stop them until the Web/Mind is activated.

"So how long will that be? We don't have all day, you know," Elmo said.

We need five of your hours. Approximately. The Grralath will be here before that.

"I can feel them," Amy said suddenly.

"What's that, Amy?" Earl asked, looking down at the girl.

She had a strange look on her face. She closed her eyes and then opened them again. "I can feel them," she repeated.

The Grralath will come to destroy the Council.

"I can feel them. They're coming!" Amy shouted. "Remember when I knew they were at Blue Water? Then again on the beach before we made it to Walter's? I can feel their presence—and they are definitely coming!"

You can help us know. They will come here. They search for the Web/Mind.

"Wait a minute!" Elmo exclaimed. "They're coming here?"

**They will destroy the Council. Without the

Council there we'll be no Web/Mind. We will go aboveground. We will fight until the Web/Mind is ready,** the Council voice told them.

If there is time, it added ominously.

"Yeah! Bring out the weapons!" Earl said, high-fiving Elmo. "I say we stomp on those bugs!"

We will go aboveground. You will fight. Fight for your planet and for ours, the Council voice said.

CHAPTER 14

ESCAPE

While Earl, Elmo, and Amy were preparing to help the Kramath in their last desperate battle against the Grralath, Johnny was lying in the purple sand of the desert that covered most of Drigoonaa, looking down into a valley at a prison camp—a prison camp for Kramath.

A line of light drew a square on the valley floor. Inside the square, thousands of Kramath stood singly or massed together in groups, their mottled bodies forming clumps of drab color against the purple of the sand that spread out in all directions. Around the perimeter of the square of light, a dozen or so Grralath marched continuously, their gigantic black bodies a constant warning to the Kramath inside. At the far end of the camp was a many-faceted clump of shining silver, a Grralath ship. Beyond that there was little else to be seen. Johnny peered at the camp a moment longer and then turned to Talu.

"That's where my dad is?" Johnny asked doubtfully.

Talu, his eight long legs curled up under his oval body, communicated that that was correct. **That is what we think.**

"So how do we get him out?" Johnny asked.

We do not. You have seen. There are many guards. We must go.

"I'm not going anywhere," Johnny told the alien.

We must go, Talu insisted.

"Look, I'm not going anywhere until I get my dad out of there. You go back if you want to, but I'm not leaving!" Johnny argued.

Humans. You have seen... Talu began, but Johnny interrupted him.

"Wait, something's happening down there!" he said.

Inside the camp, a clump of Kramath were moving quickly in a tight circle. It was hard to tell what they were doing, and then Johnny realized that they were fighting. One Kramath lay on its back and another Kramath pounced on top of it while still more of the aliens rolled in bunches, kicking up clouds of purple dust.

A second later, Johnny saw one of the Grralath guards approach a slender black post sunk in the sand at one corner of the square of light. It raised its front leg and touched the post before scuttling forward into the camp. Another Grralath followed it, and within seconds, two of the fighting Kramath lay dead beneath their captors, while the others cowered some distance away, keeping a discreet margin of safety between themselves and the deadly Great Grralath Spiders.

Whatever the fight had been about, the Grralath had settled it. And moments later they exited the camp, once again touching the post, and took up positions outside the line of light that corralled the prisoners.

That's when Johnny saw his father!

"There's my dad!" he exclaimed in a low voice.

A lone human emerged from a doorway that had opened up in the ground, and approached the dead Kramath. The spiders crowded around the human and touched him, communicating to him, pistoning up and down on their eight legs excitedly. He raised his arms and walked among them. Whatever they were talking about, it seemed to have a calming effect on the alien spiders as many of those jerking up and down began to settle and become still.

"Talu, that's my dad," Johnny said.

I know. He is a friend of the Kramath now.

"Yeah, that's him. He could be friends with anybody—even giant spiders from another world," Johnny said with a grim smile on his face.

You also are a friend of the Kramath. Talu said.

Johnny didn't answer right away. He turned and examined the alien crouching in the sand next to him. It was definitely ugly. But Talu was all right. He patted the giant arachnoid on its smooth back and nodded.

"Yeah, I guess I am," Johnny agreed. But you might not think so, old spider buddy, once I tell you my plan, he thought a moment later.

"Hi, spider-face, nice place you got here!" Johnny shouted as Talu pushed him from behind.

The Grralath standing guard near the black post that seemed to control the force field around the camp went deadly still. Its mandibles clicked once. That was the sound that everyone who ever met one of these big boys never heard twice. They were usually spider bait by the time those massive jaws clicked shut again.

Talu butted into Johnny with the front of his body so that he careened forward and sprawled on the sand. The Grralath took a few silent steps forward. It was now Talu's turn to freeze. As Johnny lay on the ground, he could only imagine the conversation going on between the two aliens, once part of the same world, now—and for millennia past—deadly enemies.

The plan was deceptively simple—maybe *stupid* was a better word, Johnny thought to himself. Talu would lead the human forward to the prison camp. He would communicate to the Grralath that he was a renegade Kramath and wanted to join them. That alone would be enough to cause some confusion, as Talu could not remember ever once hearing of a renegade Kramath.

The Grralath moved a step or two closer to Talu. Johnny could hear its legs grinding into the purple sand. Its eye lights blinked ominously. Johnny thought for a moment that he could feel the monster's gaze resting on him, evaluating the situation. C'mon, you ugly bug, buy it! Johnny pleaded silently.

As a token of goodwill, Talu brought the human prisoner, whom he had stolen from his superiors. Once Talu had convinced the Grralath and they were being led inside the camp, all Johnny had to do was reach up and punch the button on the post that controlled the force field, run in and get his dad, and—

"Talu! No!" Johnny yelled.

In one lightning-fast move, the guard pounced on the young Kramath, and Talu was locked in a desperate struggle. Rolling over in the sand, tangled in the legs of the monster Grralath, Talu was fighting for his life. Johnny glanced around quickly. The other Grralath guards were at the other end of the camp. At least they had timed it right. Johnny jumped to his feet and ran to the control post.

The Kramath in the camp had noticed the fight and were beginning to move in Johnny's direction. He was about to punch the button that he knew was there. He stopped—there were about fifteen buttons, blinking madly in different colors. He had to hurry! Talu was giving his life in a stupid attempt to save Johnny's father.

Johnny looked back to see the Grralath snapping its giant mandibles at Talu while the young Kramath held it off as best he could. The young human then turned back to the post and started pushing buttons. Out of the corner of his eye he saw a flash of black. The other Grralath were coming at full speed.

He punched a button and a geyser of sand erupted in the middle of the camp—wrong button! He jabbed at another one and a low humming noise accompanied by a vibration under his feet began. The force field was not affected.

The Grralath had Talu down and was raising its jaws for the last jab and tear. Johnny closed his eyes and starting hitting the buttons as fast as he could.

"Hit the bottom button twice, fast," a voice said. Johnny looked up. It was his dad, Major Coombs. Johnny smiled and his father yelled at him, smiling back. "Hit it now—twice, fast, Coombs!" he bellowed.

Johnny did as he was told. There was a crackling sound, and the force field ceased to exist. He looked up and was almost trampled by a stampede of rampaging Kramath! They poured out of the camp and attacked the guards. Johnny jumped out of the way, looking behind him just in time to see the one that had been about to kill Talu being pulled down by at least a dozen angry Kramath. He couldn't see Talu—he could only hope that the brave young alien was all right.

Then he was plucked off his feet by strong hands and lifted onto the hard, shell-like back of a Kramath.

His dad was there behind him, smiling at him—thinner, with more lines in his face, his uniform in rags, but it was him!

"You did good, son. I'm glad to see you," he said. Then the Kramath they were riding communicated with them.

It is your eggling? it said.

"Yes, Puow. My eggling," Major Coombs replied.

"Now what do we do, Dad?" Johnny asked, looking around at the Kramath. They had separated and surrounded the Grralath guards but were not trying to kill them.

"Puow?" his father asked the alien.

We must save our brothers the Grralath, and then go to the Web/Mind.

As if on a signal, all the Grralath attacked at once, charging at the Kramath ringing them. In seconds, it was over and the Grralath lay dead.

We could not save them, the alien named Puow said. Johnny thought he could almost hear sadness in the alien voice.

"Then let's get out of here!" Major Coombs called out, and the army of Kramath began to move away from the camp.

CHAPTER 15

LOOKOUTS

"I don't see anything," Elmo said, his shoes crunching in the purple sand as he spit wind-blown dust out of his mouth. He reached up and brushed his right ear. The Kramath had rigged some kind of communication device out of the webbing they used for everything. They had wound it around his and Earl's ears so that they could speak directly to Amy without having to go through one of the Kramath scouts that ranged around them, dotting the violet landscape with their mottled, oval bodies.

"Me neither. Amy, are you sure they're out here?" Earl asked. He shaded his eyes with one hand and scanned the horizon. It was hot and the sweat was pouring down his face, streaking the purple dust with ribbons of black. Unconsciously he touched the small machine that he wore on his belt. The Kramath had told him that it was some kind of force field. It would activate in the presence of Grralath, but only if they made a move to harm him. Secretly, Earl wished they would find one. He would love to see what the thing could do.

Back at the Kramath base, Amy looked into the Web hanging in the air before her and nodded. "Yeah, you guys. They're out there. They're right around there somewhere, so be careful. There's a whole lot of them—I can feel it," she answered them.

One of the Kramath scuttled up to Earl as he climbed a small rise to get a better view.

The wind is blowing, it communicated to him.

Earl spun around at the voice in his head. "I told you guys not to sneak up on me like that. Dude! You scare me to death when you do that!" he told the alien breathlessly.

Apologies. The wind blows, it repeated.

Earl rolled his eyes and broke contact with the alien. No matter how many times it happened, he didn't think he would ever get used to that mind talk the way Amy and Elmo did. He just didn't like those bugs talking to him without moving their lips. He laughed. Of course, the things didn't have any lips, so it wasn't really their fault. Still, he didn't like the way they were always sneaking up on him and touching him. It just made him nervous. And he was nervous enough anyway.

He and Elmo were out scouting for signs of the Grralath army that Amy, with her sixth sense, and the Kramath, with their weird Web technology, said was coming. The problem was, they hadn't seen a sign of it.

He walked up to Elmo and shook his head. "News flash, Elmo. The wind is blowing. I just got that from one of our pals back there," he told his friend, jerking his thumb back at the main body of Kramath scouts.

The wind had been blowing off and on since they had left the Kramath base. The sky was tinged with purple as gusts of wind blew dust from the desert floor high into the air.

"Duh," Elmo responded sarcastically, pursing his lips.

"You see anything?" Earl asked.

"Nothing. You'd think it would be pretty hard to hide a whole army of giant killer spiders," Elmo commented, spitting again. "I hope this purple sand isn't poisonous or anything," he added.

"You know what I think? I think that the Grralath army heard that the Spider-Killers were here and they just ran home to their ugly mommies," Earl said, laughing.

"Especially when they heard *I* was here,"

Elmo said, planting his fists on his hips.

"Yeah, they went home to get their grandmas to take care of you, Stinky," Earl teased.

"I thought we were going to drop the 'Stinky' stuff!" Elmo complained.

"We tried to, but you found us," Earl shot back at him.

Elmo was about to respond when one of the Kramath scuttled up to him and touched him. Elmo nodded and the Kramath scuttled away, its six legs sinking to the first joint in a deep sand well.

"What'd he say, Elmo?" Earl asked.

"He said the wind was blowing—a storm is coming. Something like that," Elmo informed him.

"So what does that mean?" Earl asked.

"We have to get back to the base," Elmo told him.

"Dude, how can you stand those things touching you all the time? I just can't stand it. It gives me the creeps," Earl said, trudging up the slope of a high dune.

Elmo, walking beside him, stumbled forward in the sand and almost fell. Righting himself, he shrugged. "You get used to it, I guess," he said.

"What do you say we take a peek over this

dune here for good measure and then head back," Earl suggested.

"Whatever you say, fellow Spider-Killer," Elmo answered, smiling.

"I don't think I'll ever get used to it," Earl said as they climbed to the top of the small mountain of purple sand. "If you ask me, a bug is a bug is a bug. Nice bugs, mean bugs, they all deserve to be stepped on. Especially when they start messing with the good old U.S.A. You know what I would like to do..." he continued.

The words never made it out of his mouth. A huge black shape rose over the crest of the dune, and Earl and Elmo stopped in their tracks. Standing before them was a Great Spider.

A small hissing sound rose from the sand cascading down the slope as the Grralath flexed its many-jointed legs and crept toward them.

Earl touched the small force-field-bearing machine that the Kramath had given him. "Okay, machine, now's your chance—do your stuff," he said quietly.

"And do it fast," Elmo added.

The Grralath crept closer. No force field zapped the fearsome creature. One leg was raised out of the sand, and then another, as the great arachnoid moved ever closer to the two humans. Elmo and Earl took a step back. The Great Spider's eye lights seemed to be regarding them intently.

Earl tapped the machine on his hip. The Grralath continued to advance. It stopped and then lowered itself on its powerful legs. The boys clearly heard the death click of its fearsome mandibles.

"Zap it, Earl, don't be shy! Give it a good one," Elmo urged.

"I'm trying—the stupid thing isn't working!" Earl cried.

Amy's voice rang in their ears. "Get out of there, you guys!"

"Thanks for the advice," Elmo said under his breath.

And the Grralath pounced!

Elmo and Earl both saw it rise off the ground and fly toward them. There was nowhere for them to run. The Great Spider's body blocked out the sun of Drigoonaa as it came at them, its legs spread out like long spears ready to tear them apart, its giant jaws clicking and slavering, hungering for the death of the two humans.

CHAPTER 16

TRANSFORMATIONS

BBZzzzzzzzzzzzzzz!

The giant arachnoid's legs curled up and it flew backward as if a giant hand had swatted it away from Earl and Elmo. It landed on its back and spasmed, shudders running through its legs and body until it finally lay still in the purple sand.

The two boys stared in shocked silence at the body of the giant spider. Then Earl turned to Elmo. He held up his hand and Elmo smacked it with his own. "Cool!" they cried in unison. "Score one for our side!"

Behind them, the swishing of many legs on fine sand signaled the arrival of the Kramath scouts. They surrounded the Grralath and began to drag it away.

"Elmo, Earl, are you all right?" Amy shouted at them.

"Ow! What are you trying to do, blow out my

107

eardrums?" Elmo shouted back, covering his Web receiver with his hand.

"Uhh, sorry. I guess you're all right."

"Yeah, we're okay, but one ugly creepy-crawler is definitely not. Did you see that?" Elmo asked.

"Yeah, that was pretty cool," Amy answered. "You know—there's a big sandstorm heading your way, you guys. You might want to—"

"Elmo, could you come here for a minute. You might, uh, want to check this out," Earl said right then from the top of the dune.

"Yeah, yeah, we know all about the storm. We'll be back after we off a few more spiders," Elmo answered absently as he climbed up to stand next to Earl.

"You might want to talk to them about that," Earl said, motioning with his hand out at the desert.

The wind was blowing harder along the crest of the dune. Elmo shaded his eyes with one hand and covered his mouth with the other. The desert was black.

And it was moving!

As far as the eye could see, it was covered with Grralath, a huge army of certain death for the Kramath and their allies, the human race.

"Uh, Amy, umm, put out the welcome mat. I

think we're coming home," Elmo said.

"I think you'd better," Amy said, trying to keep the fear out of her voice. "And don't bring any big black eight-legged friends with you."

Elmo and Earl looked at each other and raced down the slope to where the Kramath scouts were still dragging the Grralath across the sand.

"Hey, you guys! Wait up! Wait for us!" They cried.

They caught up to the Kramath just as the alien spiders were forming a wide circle around the still Grralath. They moved out slowly, the circle taking shape with each of the Kramath touching one leg to the Kramath next to them until the Grralath was surrounded.

"I've seen this before," Elmo whispered to Earl. "It's kind of like a funeral."

Earl nodded, watching intently as the wind whipped across the dry plain on which they were standing. At first he heard a low noise, like a humming or a grinding sound. A shot of light ran though each of the Kramath forming the circle, buzzing along their bodies so quickly that Earl wasn't sure if he had seen it at all. Then the Kramath began to scuttle inward, closing the distance between themselves and the Great Spider. They continued moving in on the form of their enemy until the two humans could no longer see the Great Spider—only the mass of Kramath that covered it.

"That's a funeral?" Earl scoffed.

The mass of Kramath began to rise, slowly levitating into the air and dropping to one side until the Great Spider revealed itself in their midst, still and majestic, its black body gleaming dully in the light of its home world.

"Watch out!" Earl and Elmo cried at the same time. But the Kramath seemed unconcerned. The Grralath was making no move to attack them. Instead, it reached out one leg and laid it on the body of the nearest Kramath. The long spike-leg rested there for a moment and then was removed. The Great Spider turned toward Earl and Elmo. As they watched, the huge black arachnoid shuffled toward them. They stood rooted to the ground as it approached, its long legs sinking into the sand. When it was no more than five feet away, it stopped and lowered itself to the ground.

"What is going on?" Earl asked.

At that moment, one of the Kramath scuttled toward Earl, but the human backed up and waved it away. "Talk to this guy if you want to talk," he said, pointing at Elmo. Elmo laughed and stepped forward. The Kramath touched him, and Elmo nodded. A second later he was walking toward the Great Spider.

"Elmo, you geek, what are you doing?" Earl asked.

"It's okay, they've done something to it. It's—I guess it's tame," Elmo informed him. Then the boy reached out and touched the Great Spider's shiny black body. A small shudder seemed to wind its way through the monster's body, but that was the spider's only visible reaction to the human's contact.

The wind was definitely increasing in intensity. Elmo waved Earl over, and the other boy approached the unmoving form of the Great Spider much more cautiously than his friend had.

"This is our ride home, dude," Elmo informed him, pulling himself up on the Great Spider's back. "It'll be a lot faster, and the rest of the Kramath are staying here to try and hold off the Grralath for a while."

Earl looked at Elmo and shook his head in confusion. "Ride a Great Spider like it was a pony? And these guys," he motioned at the Kramath gathered around, "they're going to stay here and do what? That's a whole army of Grralath out there," Earl protested.

"Yeah, they're pretty stupid," Elmo laughed. "And you can stay here with them if you want. Me, I'm heading back."

Earl looked around and rushed toward the

Grralath just as it began to raise itself up on its long legs. "Wait, I'm coming—I'm coming!" Earl said as he reached out a hand to Elmo, who hauled him up onto the Grralath's back.

When they were situated, they heard the Grralath's voice in their heads. **Humans are prepared?** it asked. Or ordered, it was hard to tell.

"Uh, yeah, ready as we'll ever be," Earl said. The Great Spider took off so fast that the two boys almost went flying off its back. They quickly learned to lean forward into the spider's movements, and were soon whipping across the desert in the direction of the Kramath base.

"Did you get all of this, Amy?" Elmo asked, cupping his hand over his webbed ear.

"I got it. I don't believe it, but I got it," Amy's voice sounded in his ear.

"That makes three of us," Earl put in. It was hard to tell from the Grralath's voice, but Earl was sure that the Great Spider was having as hard a time believing what was going on as he and Elmo were.

And that didn't make him very happy. Not happy at all.

CHAPTER 17

ALIEN ARMIES

By the time they made it back to the Kramath base, the wind was blowing so hard that the boys had to cover their faces with their shirts to keep the purple dust from blinding them. The entranceway to a network of tunnels opened before them and the Grralath sped into the deep underground. Behind them, the doorway closed. The glow in the tunnel brightened enough to allow them to see.

The Grralath seemed to know where it was going, as if it were being pulled along by an unseen hand, and within minutes, they were back in what served the Kramath as their control center. Amy instinctively backed away from the huge Grralath, despite the fact that she had seen the transformation of the fearsome giant spider by the Kramath.

"It's okay, Amy, this one has been taken care of. It's those others we have to worry about,"

Elmo said, jumping off the Grralath and pointing at the glowing Web monitor. The web showed a purple chaos of dust and then, out of the dust, the army of the Grralath advanced, row upon row of the immense black spiders, marching forward, coming to destroy the Council Kramath—coming to destroy the Web/Mind!

"And they don't look very happy," Earl threw in.

"What's with this storm? How long is it supposed to last?" Elmo asked Amy.

The girl shrugged, her braces glinting in the soft glow of the control center. "They said that the sandstorms usually don't last long, they blow through and then—" Amy didn't finish. On the Web monitor they could see that the storm was already abating, the purple dust slowly filtering back down to the desert floor. And as it settled, the defenders of the Web/Mind were revealed, a pitifully thin line of Kramath standing between them and the Grralath onslaught.

"So I don't mean to rush you guys, but shouldn't you get this Web/Mind thing happening already?" Earl asked.

The Council Kramath voice boomed out over their heads. **We are almost ready,** it said.

"Almost, almost! Haven't you guys ever

heard the one about horseshoes and hand grenades?" Elmo asked impatiently.

No, the Council voice answered. **What are horseshoes and hand grenades?**

"About the only things where 'almost' counts," Elmo told it.

The Council voice did not respond.

"I guess they didn't get it," Amy said.

"They didn't get it, but those guys are about to," Earl said, pointing at the Web monitor.

It showed the advancing Grralath about to crash into the Kramath defenders. The Kramath held their ground and the Grralath picked up speed, spreading out a little. The distance between them continued to close. Earl and Amy and Elmo held their breath. The line of Kramath advanced a little, and suddenly the Grralath were on them, tearing at the Kramath and scattering them. The Grralath ripped into the Kramath with their fearsome mandibles and overpowered them through sheer numbers.

And somehow, the Kramath line held. It wouldn't hold for long, however. Amy turned and looked at the Grralath that had carried Earl and Elmo back to the Kramath base. It stood in a corner of the room, still as stone, or so she thought. Then she noticed that it was moving, pistoning up and down slightly.

"Amy, have you heard anything from Johnny?" Earl asked her.

She spun around. "Uh, no—I just, I have to believe he is all right," she said, trying to smile.

"I hope he's doing better than we are," Earl announced grimly.

Amy looked back at the transformed Grralath. It was definitely getting excited. Could the Kramath be wrong? Was it getting back to its old self?

"Council, shouldn't we tie the Grralath up or something?" Amy asked out loud.

Our brother is worried. Nothing more. We create the Web/Mind.

Earl and Elmo breathed big sighs of relief. "It's about time!" Earl shouted.

The line of Kramath defenders was weakening and pulling apart in places, littering the desert with a few huge black corpses and many smaller mottled ones. Grralath poured through the holes in the line and began digging, throwing up purple sand in all directions, looking for the entranceway to the base.

CHAPTER 18

HORSESHOES AND HAND GRENADES

"Honey, they're home!" Elmo yelled.

Then the Grralath stopped. Something shot over their heads, a large silver ship! A Grralath ship!

"Oh, great!" Earl exclaimed. "Air support!"

The ship started firing thin needles of light that blew clouds of purple sand and rock into the air wherever they touched down.

But it wasn't firing at the Kramath—it was firing at the Great Spiders!

Then a voice sounded through the room. "Hey, you guys! I don't know if you can hear me. It's Johnny with my dad. We thought you might need a little help!"

Amy and Earl and Elmo looked at each other and cheered, jumping into the air. "I knew it! I knew he would be okay!" Earl shouted.

The ship made another low pass over the Grralath lines, firing randomly, and a small army of Kramath came into view on the Web monitor. They attacked the Grralath from behind as the huge spiders got over their shock and once again began searching for a way into the Kramath base.

The three kids turned from the monitor at a strange sound. The Council Kramath were ranged in a circle, all of them pumping up and down, while a strange whistling sound echoed through the room. Beyond them, the captive Grralath mimicked their movements, pistoning up and down in time with the Council Kramath.

"You guys! We could be in trouble!" Amy announced. The boys turned back to look at the Web monitor. The Grralath had found the opening to the base and were using their front legs and powerful jaws to try and pry the door open. It looked as if they almost had it open when Johnny, in the Grralath craft, made another low sweep and blasted them with a hot spike of burning white light.

"Good one, Johnny!" Amy shouted.

But more Grralath took the places of the dead. Johnny made another pass, blasted some more, and still they kept coming.

"Come on, you guys, hurry!" Amy shrieked.

The door to the underground base was wrenched open at last, and the kids watched the Web monitor silently as the mammoth black forms poured into the entry.

The Council Kramath's movements increased in intensity and the whistling sound grew louder. At the same time, something heavy hit the door to the control room, filling the room with a resounding *boom!* Suddenly, light erupted from the Council Kramath, a huge shining golden light that shot to the ceiling and lit the chamber as it rolled and condensed like a cloud above the spiders' heads.

Boom! The door to the control room began to buckle under the repeated blows of the monstrous spiders outside.

The golden light filling the room began to coalesce into the form of a Web, a bright shining Web that was beautiful to look at but also terrible. It hovered over them all and then began to settle back toward the floor as the Kramath's movements became more and more frantic. Somehow the kids knew that when the shining golden Web reached the floor and surrounded the Council Kramath, who had brought it into being as a weapon to save their planet, the power of the Web/Mind would be unleashed!

That's when the captive Grralath struck!

Either the transformation had not been successful, or the sight of the Web/Mind had

driven it madder than before. Whatever the
reason, the Grralath struck out furiously, rip-
ping into the nearest Council Kramath just as
the light of the Web/Mind touched its smooth,
shiny back. The golden Web froze in midair as
the Grralath opened the belly of the Kramath
and spread its guts over the floor. Other
Kramath—guards and servants of the Council
Kramath—pounced on the Grralath, bringing
it down as quickly as they could. But they were
not fast enough. The Council Kramath that
had been attacked was dead. The Web/Mind
was frozen.

Boom! The Grralath outside were smashing
the door to pieces, and they would do so until
they were all dead if that's what it took to
destroy the Web/Mind.

**We are finished. There are not enough of
us to complete the shaping of the Web/Mind,**
the Council voice said.

"Noooooo!" the kids yelled as one. It couldn't
end like this. They had been through too much.
Too much depended on this. It couldn't be—it
couldn't.

Amy walked over to the place in the circle
that had recently been occupied by the Council
Kramath.

"Elmo, Earl—come here. Hold my hands.
Join the circle—we can do this. I can do it.

With your energy and mine, I'll join us to the Web/Mind!" she cried.

"What are you talking about? We're not spiders, we're people!" Earl protested.

The door to the control room began to bend inward. The Grralath were forcing their way through.

"Just come here!" Amy yelled. "Hold my hands!"

Elmo and Earl looked at the door. It would be down in a matter of seconds. They looked at each other and shrugged. Amy's mom *had* been a psychic on TV, after all.

They ran and joined her, each of them grabbing one of her hands. Amy closed her eyes. They looked at her and then at the door. Were those Grralath coming through? Their long legs and giant black bodies tangling with each other to get inside—to kill!

Sweat ran down Amy's face as she struggled to join with the Kramath and bring the Web/Mind down. She could hear their voices. Not the voices that they used to communicate to the humans, but their true voices as they pulled the Web/Mind into a whole, as they concentrated and focused it. And her mind joined theirs.

The door went down and the Great Spiders flooded into the room. The Kramath not engaged in the process of the Web/Mind tried to stop them, but they were no match for the fearsome Great Ones, and they were tossed aside like toys.

That was all the time that the Council Kramath and the kids from Earth needed, however.

The Grralath were no match for the Web/Mind!

The golden Web descended and touched the bodies of the Kramath and the two boys and one girl—and it erupted into a ball of golden light that filled the chamber! The Grralath stopped and pistoned up and down once or twice. They were trying to get back out the door when the golden fire caught them and knocked them to the floor, where they stayed, unmoving.

The fire then moved on, erupting through the walls and ceiling, growing larger and larger until it appeared on the desert floor above the control room and spread itself out, growing ever larger and ever brighter, flashing out and stopping Grralath in their tracks with bursts of bright golden flame that left them still and lifeless on the purple sand. And still it continued to grow until the Web that it became covered the whole planet and shone in the darkness of space!

The Grralath were defeated!

Amy and Earl and Elmo stood breathlessly in the control room. "Wow, that was pretty cool!" Elmo said.

"Oh, yeah, we should do that more often," Earl commented.

Amy didn't say anything, she could only stare at the Web monitor. It showed Earth, and around the beautiful blue-green ball hanging against the black velvet of endless space was a golden Web!

"Look at that, you guys," she said. Then she fell in a faint on the floor. Elmo and Earl rushed to her and knelt down beside her.

"Are you okay, Amy? Are you all right?" Elmo asked anxiously.

As Earl patted her hand and fanned her face, Amy's eyes fluttered open and she said something they couldn't hear.

"What was that, Amy?" Earl asked, putting his ear next to her mouth.

"Horseshoes and hand grenades," she said. Then she laughed.

EPILOGUE

Johnny Coombs dreamed of giant spiders.

He saw them everywhere. Their eye lights flashed messages of death and destruction as the monstrous jaws tore and ripped at everything he had ever known. He was back in Blue Water and he was surrounded. The horrible spiders were closing in on him. He spun to the right and then to the left, using every trick he had ever learned during football practice.

But there was nowhere to run!

The spiders crept closer. He could hear their mandibles clicking, the sound of death. He took one step back—and then another. Then a thought occurred to him. If I can't go left or right or backward or forward, the only way to go is up, he thought. And up he went, his whole body growing and expanding until he towered over the spiders and they became nothing more than small, insignificant black dots against a carpet of green grass.

He raised his foot and smiled. Who's afraid of a couple of little spiders? he thought. Then he brought his boot down and ground the spiders into the Earth with a satisfying crunching sound.

"Take that, spider-brains!" he said out loud.

Then he woke up. He opened his eyes and for a second he wasn't sure where he was—then he remembered. He was home. He was on the Earth—and the Earth was safe.

He sat on the edge of the bed and put his bare feet on the floor. Across the room, Elmo and Earl slept peacefully.

Once the Grralath had been defeated by the Web/Mind on Drigoonaa, the Kramath had been able to deploy it on Earth as well. Soon afterward, the Council Kramath had used it to send Johnny and his dad, Amy, Earl, and Elmo back to Earth.

Major Holloway sure had a funny look on his face when he saw them all materialize out of a ball of red-orange light at the entrance to the Los Angeles Coliseum. His men had drawn their weapons for a minute, and Johnny had thought that they were all going to get shot until Holloway had recognized them.

"When that ship of theirs just took off without any warning, we thought we'd had it," he told them all later, when they had had some food and were relaxing in a room that the major requisitioned for them. "Then we just loaded up those souped-up water pistols those spiders had shown us how to make and we hit the beach. We had them on the run, too—for a minute. Then those webbed ones took over, and of course they weren't afraid of water, or anything else. It was awful..." the major trailed off, not wanting to talk about the fight with the webbed ones.

"Then that Web thingy appeared in the sky," he began again, after a long breath. "And those big, ugly creepy-crawlers just started getting zapped left and right. The webbed ones came to right afterward, like they were waking up from a long dream. We had a heck of a time keeping them from tearing those spiders apart with their bare hands.

"Of course, then your buddies—those other bugs—appeared out of nowhere and we just let them do their work. They gathered all those big, ugly black ones up in heaps and that Web thing started zapping them into who knows where—they just started disappearing, which was fine with me," the Major added, twisting his mustache.

Johnny got up and padded to the window looking out over what was left of downtown Los Angeles. The tests that the Grralath had run on their dehydrating machine had wrecked the place, but that didn't really matter—the human race had all the time in the world to fix things up. What did matter was that when Johnny looked up, the Web of the Grralath that had hung over the world was almost gone. Only a few stray strands, glinting in the sun, were all that was left to remind anyone that they had been there at all.

He stepped across the cold floor and picked his pillow up off his bed. Across the room, Earl and Elmo were still sleeping. Amy had a room of her own next door. Then he hurled his pillow at the sleeping form of Earl.

"Hey what the— What's going on?" the boy mumbled as he sat straight up, pushing a handful of black hair out of his face.

"Time to get up, sleepyhead—you too, Elmo," Johnny yelled gleefully.

"Oh, shut up! What's a guy got to do to get a little sleep around here? Save the world or something?" Elmo said sleepily, rubbing his eyes.

"C'mon, you guys, get up! Don't you remember? Today's the day we get our medals!" Johnny informed them.

"Well, when you get mine, don't forget to say thank you," Elmo said, stretching and yawning.

Johnny and Earl looked at each other and smiled. "Oh, get up, Stinky!" they yelled as their pillows flew across the room and hit him in the head, one after the other.

The crowd in the Coliseum was huge. The dehydrating machine of the Grralaths was still there. It had been decided that it would be left up as a reminder of what had happened.

Beneath the giant machine, Elmo Dodd, Johnny Coombs, Amy Rasmussen, and Earl Two-Sticks fidgeted nervously. They were the Spider-Killers, the kids from Blue Water, Washington, who had saved the world.

"Dude, you look pretty stupid in those fancy clothes," Earl teased Johnny, nudging him in the ribs. They had had to get dressed up for the occasion and they were all uncomfortable in their new clothes.

"I think he looks nice," Amy said, smiling at Johnny.

"Thanks, Amy," Johnny told the girl. "You look pretty nice yourself," he added.

"I think all three of you look ridiculous," Elmo put in.

Earl was about to grab him for a quick round of super-noogies when Major Holloway and Johnny's dad stepped up to a makeshift podium next to the kids. The crowd gathered in the

Coliseum roared. Major Holloway took out four medals from a box he carried and showed them to the crowd.

"For service to Earth, above and beyond—" Major Holloway began.

Johnny smiled at the others. *"Way* beyond," he joked.

"The call of duty. The people of Earth award you these medals," the major finished. The crowd roared their approval once again, and the major pinned a medal to each of their chests.

Johnny looked at his dad, and Major Coombs winked at him. Not far away, Mr. and Mrs. Two-Sticks were beaming at Earl. Johnny knew that Elmo's plan was to go back north to find his mom as soon as possible. It was the same for Amy, she wanted to find her mom— and Johnny knew she would, he just knew it.

He turned to the others and held out his hand.

"Spider-Killers forever," he said loudly, grinning from ear to ear.

The others laid their hands on his.

"Spider-Killers forever!" they repeated, laughing.

The crowd cheered.

Also available from
Random House Children's Publishing:

THE WEB, VOLUME ONE

By
TOM HUGHES